LIFE
DRAWING

LIFE
DRAWING

A NOVEL BY
Michael Grumley

Foreword by
EDMUND WHITE

Afterword by
GEORGE STAMBOLIAN

GROVE WEIDENFELD
New York

Published by Grove Weidenfeld
A division of Grove Press, Inc.
841 Broadway
New York, NY 10003–4793

Published in Canada by General Publishing Company, Ltd.

Library of Congress Cataloging-in-Publication Data

Grumley, Michael.
Life drawing / Michael Grumley. — 1st ed.
p.   cm.
ISBN 0-8021-1438-5
I. Title.
PS3557.R834L54   1991
813'.54—dc20   91-8647
                                          CIP

Manufactured in the United States of America
Printed on acid-free paper
Designed by Irving Perkins Associates
First Edition 1991
1   3   5   7   9   10   8   6   4   2

for Robert Ferro

Foreword

Sex has gotten a bad name recently, but this book reminds us that sex is something worth dying for. It's rare that we read a book by a handsome man; most writers are so homely that only the best of the lot rate being called "distinguished." But Michael Grumley was both handsome and manly, and this autobiographical novel reveals that beautiful men are not like you and me. For one thing they get to be with other beauties. Their sex isn't hungry, grateful, greedy, or choked with emotion. It expresses emotion. Calmly. Radiantly.

But there is something even a beautiful person has in common with a desperate one if they're both intensely sexual: They feel their sexuality to be their secret, inner nature, their destiny, and alternatively something they're driven to find out. Gertrude Stein's black character Melanctha in *Three Lives* considers sex to be a form of knowledge, chastening, irresistible, and so transforming it can be thought of only as educational. That's the way I read *Life Drawing*, as the story of a beautiful young man determined to get to the bottom of this cold artesian well he's turned into.

Sex of this magnitude (sex as a vocation) can utterly change a life. An adolescent white boy from a midwestern town leaves his friends and family to float down the Mississippi (Huck with Jim) to an unforeseen life with James, a young black man in the French Quarter. The prose, which has been pleasantly discursive up till now, suddenly lowers its voice. In fact, the voice shakes with emotion, every detail is articulated with rapt pleasure, and an aching sensuousness replaces the earlier cocksureness.

No lunging equipment, no hairs in the teeth—no, this is the opposite of pornography, which replaces sex or indeed is a form of sex. By contrast this writing renders sex; it doesn't replace it. It renders the unreality of the day spent away from the four-poster bed, renders the formal, tender complicity of the lovers when they come offstage after their long tragicomedy and, smiling mildly, mingle with the groundlings. It renders the lovers' absolute certainty that they're superior to everyone, a superiority so certain it has no need to assert itself and paradoxically comes across as humility. Not since Truman Capote has anyone written so well about New Orleans, with the difference that Grumley's New Orleans isn't built up out of impeccable observations but rather given to us whole like a sword we're meant to swallow.

Friendship without sex, sex without love or even friendship—these are possibilities explored in the California section of the book, which, because of these absences, is more social than intimate, more a training period than an act of transubstantiation. For only the religious word *transubstantiation* can say what love with sex, sex with love provide—the mystic conversion of one substance into another, you into me, although outward appearances remain unchanged. This is what James and Mickey know, sexual love, and they know it with the golden calm that is perhaps the prerogative of the physically beautiful.

At the end of the book Mickey has come home; he's still just eighteen, his brothers, as foreseen, are pairing off with girls, but Mickey—who's been a whore, a failed movie actor, an artist's model, a factory worker, a kept boy, even a jailbird for one night—has changed completely. He's learned the severe, taxing duties of sex.

I never knew Michael Grumley well, even though I spent many evenings with him. His lover, Robert Ferro, had a much more aggressive personality. It was Robert who was full of gossip, who would flare up, who felt slighted, who offered love and advice, who made things happen, who demanded *details*. Michael was steadier but also more detached, sometimes almost benignly goofy with detachment. Both he and Robert were handsome men, virile, confident, but Michael lived in his own world, camouflaged by his unfocused smile, his generalized sounds of affirmation, his vague bonhomie.

Perhaps he'd learned that in the gay world at least his powerful body with its massive chest, broad shoulders, tiny waist, neat butt, big legs would do all the social work for him. He purred up in his big Cadillac of a body and dozed or daydreamed inside. Not that he cultivated a gay look typical of the period, the late seventies and early eighties, when I knew him best. Granted, he had the regulation mustache, but he also had a ponytail, baggy clothes, a wide, smiling face, a receding forehead. He seemed more like Jack Nicholson without the satanism, or like a certain kind of Vietnam vet, the kind who was a crack paratrooper and still has the body and confidence to show for it but whom disillusionment has turned into a homemade Buddhist, an artist, a skeptic, and a loner. Maybe he was a man who liked people but didn't need them.

All he needed was his marriage to Robert and his adventures with those black men he and Robert both loved but seldom talked about. They lived on the Upper West Side in a big, comfortable apartment within easy striking distance of Harlem. Michael wrote a regular column for the *New York Native* about his uptown beat. And Robert and Michael had both told me they had black and Puerto Rican lovers. Not *lots* of lovers, not commodities or fetishes. Robert, for instance, had one lover for many years. He had his lover, and he had his husband, Michael.

They were inseparable, so much so that we called them the Ferro-Grumleys, as though they were an aristocratic English family. If they were serious about sexual love (not with each other but with those lovers we never met), they were equally serious about only one other thing: art, their artistic life together. Perhaps they were the last genuine bohemians. Neither of them ever seemed to work except at fiction or unpaid journalism, but neither of them would have dreamed of doing the things the rest of us had to do to scrape by—editing, magazine writing, ghostwriting, teaching. They thought the world owed them a living, as it probably did, considering how beautifully they wrote and how little time they would have to live.

We had Italy in common. We'd all three lived in Rome, though I hadn't known them then. We all spoke Italian and cared about food and clothes and street life with a degree of seriousness that struck other Americans as frivolous. Italy had also taught us that money isn't everything and that poor bohemians have more fun.

I never saw them at the New York bars I went to or at the baths, no more than I saw there another friend, Robert Mapplethorpe. Too white. My gay world was too white for them.

I saw Mapplethorpe over dinner or at his place. The Ferro-Grumleys I saw at our own literary teas, the meetings of our gay writers' club, The Violet Quill.

Michael's vagueness dropped away when he read his work to us. He read in a low, manly, highly intelligent voice (a voice can be intelligent if it's supple, haunted by inverted commas, impatient with the frustrating linear nature of speech yet reconciled to the exigencies of performance, or if it's a medium for other, invading voices). He was a grown-up, a father. He would have been *our* father if he hadn't been so self-protectingly abstracted, mysterious, genial. Perhaps he was genial to cool off the white-hot rages he was capable of (he was a reformed alcoholic). In The Violet Quill days he was working on a text in which, as in *Life Drawing*, the Mississippi made an appearance, an exciting, rotting highway to elsewhere. What wasn't in that version was James. James was his secret, his ideal. When at the end of his life he gave his secret away he had to depart, just as Lohengrin must go away after he pronounces his own name.

We were all surprised that Michael was the only member of our group not to publish his fiction, since we considered him to be, if not the most talented, then at least the most accomplished writer amongst us (perhaps he was also the most talented, but each of us secretly coveted that honor for himself).

Shortly before Michael's death Robert published his own *Second Son* and was very bitter about the bad review it received in the *New York Times*. He said, "They're never going to give us a chance, Ed." I invited Robert to join me in France, and I made hotel reservations for us in Belle-Île. I wanted to cheer him up. I said we'd rent bikes, but he said, "I don't think you realize what bad shape I'm in. Well, we'll be like two old duffers just duffering around," and that image seemed to comfort him. He told me he was working on Michael's novel, *Life Drawing*, polishing it. Robert knew that editing Michael's book would be his last creative effort. Just before he was to come to Belle-Île he died.

Now the Ferro-Grumleys are buried together in a grave overlooking the Hudson; five of the original eight members of The Violet Quill are dead. The other seven had all published their books; at last the eighth is enshrined in print as well. The idea of a shrine may be too cold and static to capture the rustling purity of this book, so true to its ambiguous title (I picture life being drawn up the pipette or sap drawn up the branch). No, think of this book as a tree growing up out of Michael's manly and enigmatic heart.

EDMUND WHITE
April 1991

Love is a babe.

—WILLIAM SHAKESPEARE

LIFE
DRAWING

The first thing I remember is dancing with my brother.

I was born inside a bend in the Mississippi River, a year after he arrived, and six months before the bombing of Pearl Harbor; born in the state of Iowa, in a placid land, but equipped with a combustible spirit. My parents, white middle-class Protestants, seemed to Franklin and me to be as happily and perfectly paired as two sugar figurines on a cake.

Franklin and I grew up listening to swing time, two toddlers in short pants performing for each other— we learned to walk to the tooting of the Dorsey Brothers, took a few faltering steps across the carpet while around us spun the lyrics of "Green Eyes," the scalloped turning rhythms of "Tangerine." Mom had a Bakelite radio in the kitchen, and in the living room a fat brown box built like a cathedral poured melody after melody through its oval doors. The music is stitched across those early years, cutting through jagged newsreel shots of men in flaming airplanes, of parachutes rippling open against the sky, of jitterbugging couples kicking back the night.

Brother musicians were the fixed stars of the wartime sky—Tommy and Jimmy Dorsey; Bing and Bob Crosby, their voices like red wine and white wine; and the sturdy nasal Eberles, singing on other stations in front of other bands, making "Fools Rush In" their own. Guy and Carmine Lombardo were venerable as Christmas trees, Les and Larry Elgart bright and sassy as their horns, the Mills Brothers soft and creamy and reassuring.

We were dusted and diapered while the sound of saxophones and clarinets and baritones swam around us: Mom sang along with the radio and at night Dad sang us his own songs and lullabies. We held each other by the hand and bounced along, while the war sputtered away in the distance; the only echo we heard was in the male camaraderie of the Big Band choruses, persuading America that war or no war, we were all one big happy family, healthy, optimistic, and strong.

Who wouldn't aspire to blend in with this sustaining choir? Jukeboxes in Mizlo's Tap and the Iowana Farms soda shop rang with the same heroic force and resiliency. What we heard rather than what we saw was the inspiration of our youth. When Mom took us to the Saturday serial at the Blackhawk Theater and we got both the Eyes and Ears of the World—as the newsreel proclaimed itself—we became giddy and overstimulated. Our delights, our consistencies, were aural.

I think we two boys were like two eggs in our safe midwestern nest, protected and coddled by circumstance. Then, a few years later, after even the wake of the war had receded, an eye snapped open in the living room, a fuzzy glare we called the Zenith, the television, and then, familiarly, as if it had been there always, the TV. The TV brought with it a complete change of perspective; its great arc moved across the country, lighting up and changing ambitions and perceptions. In my third year of grammar school the shift of focus occurred—thereafter one was able to see, every day of one's life, the living moving world in living moving black and white.

Kate Smith is the first figure I remember, her body full and buxom, her eternally white features poised above a velvet bodice, soft as a licorice gumdrop.

When we first got our round-screened set, no one was sure where it should go. It began low, sitting on the carpet like a warming fire, then Dad tried it on top of the bureau, turned slightly like an outsize family photograph. Finally, it came to rest on the coffee table, at its permanent height, just about a foot and a half off the floor. New voices and new faces came tumbling out of it in twos and threes and fours. The new brother acts had abandoned trombones and clarinets: the Four Aces and the Four Lads, the Ames Brothers and the Everly Brothers shone forth every weekend, bringing high plaintive harmonics into our 4/4 lives. Don and Phil were the siblings of the moment, handsome and wise, replacing Tommy and Jimmy, Bing and Bob. Ed Sullivan nodded and bowed, like the felt-covered plaster dog in the back window of our Nash, and introduced Elvis Presley into our lives. We sat in the twilight, in our little river town, and watched smoky figures yodel and cavort, listened to Jerry Lester tell his ancient jokes, witnessed the phenomenal creature called Dagmar strut and bounce.

Soon the desire to have a TV—which had preceded its acquisition by nearly a year—was replaced by the equally strong desire to be on it. There were boy tumblers and acrobats and occasionally singers on "Toast of the Town"—my own squeaky soprano would be the key to my success. Dreams were brought out and embellished; afternoon programming soon mesmerized the mothers and aunts of Lillienthal, and stage mothers bloomed in kitchen gardens.

5

Shortly, I too was part of a brother act. Franklin and I rehearsed a song from a Bob Hope movie, called "Buttons and Bows," over and over again, and Mom made us a pair of outfits, augmented by the stitchery of one of the women in Dad's office. Our first television appearance was made when we were nine and ten, on Cowboy Ken's afternoon show; we stood in his outdoor corral at station WOZ and sang and smiled for his audience, and for him. Cowboy Ken was a big sincere man who smelled of tobacco and pomade, and our outfits were scaled-down replicas of his own plaid shirt and shiny chaps. We wore immaculate felt cowboy hats that we charmingly doffed at the end of the number as we grinned and bowed and imagined the applause behind the camera lens.

Something very warming about that little red light. We came back and sang "The Lonesome Hobo's Lament" a few months later, and were working on "I Ain't Got No Use for the Women"—both songs learned from Dad, who had himself learned them on a dude ranch one summer. But Cowboy Ken's show was abruptly canceled. We later learned he had been packed off to the correctional facility at Sioux Falls after some impropriety with one of the little cowgirls.

I don't think we were so much shocked as disappointed that our own careers had been cut short along with his. I knew that Don and Phil Everly were the singing stars Franklin and I might have become, if only we had kept on. Like two tines on a tuning fork, they hummed with melancholy glamour. They shone like icons in the golden light of the stage, were the model of all aspiration. Later on, in high school, I would take my girlfriend Sammy to the Coliseum Ballroom whenever they appeared and sway back and forth with the enraptured crowd.

I slid into my teenage years with undiminished dreams of fame and romance, celebrity. I might never be a single, but oh what a double-act success I would make, with the right partner standing next to me up there on the bandstand . . . just like Don and Phil, Bing and Bob. I imagined myself replacing one or the other of the Brothers, stepping blithely into either pair of gleaming white bucks. I was eager for the spotlight, and jitterbugged myself into a froth of envy. Envy was a living creature, consuming me bite by bite—how I got through such nights of yearning ambition, I don't know. That aspiration I felt as an unfocused child seems to have been the main reality in my young life, seems to have propelled me straight through.

We were bred for cute. We were bred for popular. That's what made those moments on early television so wonderful, the magnified popularity of them. On TV, you were somewhere other than your own body, someone other than your own self. You confronted strangers by the thousands, all at once, and you won them over with a dazzling immediacy. I felt there was nothing more glorious than being plugged into a larger system via Cowboy Ken and his bunkhouse transmission, shining out from the remoteness of the midwest, across plains and rivers and trailer parks and subdivisions, to something wider and vaster.

Doubling up, experiences that came in pairs, seemed the rule when we were young. As a pair, we got duplicate outfits, duplicate gifts. And then a year apart another pair of brothers arrived, Dennie Lee and Christopher. The symmetry of our situation made us special, as if we older boys had been such a success that Mom and Dad had decided to replicate it with two more. What had worked for us was prescribed for them. Our little brown bears, named after two ursine brothers at the zoo and having managed to survive our squeezing torments, fell into our baby brothers' embrace those few years later. They endured, trailing behind the two of us, the four of us, ultimately losing their buzzer-growls, surviving mute into a grizzled and ragamuffin old age.

Lillienthal was then a collection of six thousand souls, and, except for the downtown section, was not so different from the sprawl of farms and farm buildings out on Five Mile Road—it had sidewalks and hedges, to be sure, and outbuildings converted to utility shacks, but the atmosphere was still rural. Across the road from where we lived was a great flowering field that belonged to a widow and her daughter, and beside it an uncleared stretch of land as thickly wooded as the frontiersmen had found it. Still, the town had neighborhoods. Ours was a few blocks wide, composed of brand-new wood-frame houses. Some of the houses, like ours, had sloping terraces, while others stood on flat land; all of them were sturdy and modest and just barely middle-class.

Mom had been a city girl, working as a typist, occasionally acting with the Blackstone Players, a theatrical group of ambitious repertoire. Dad was a country boy, attending Maquoketa College and playing football, singing in bars on weekends for beer and change. There was a double date, and then an elopement—the way we heard it, everything happened in the twinkling of an eye.

Our parents were American as they could be, and we were their sons. Dad came up out of the midwestern earth, and made his living from machines that tilled the earth. Eagle tractors and Eagle combines broke the ground we all trod: farm equipment was a product to believe in.

During the World War, he'd stayed in Iowa, part of what we were told was the necessary war effort at home; his younger brother Keith was a sailor, who might at any moment appear at our door in his glistening whites, a tall blonde on his arm, red-white-and-blue thunder crackling and snapping around him. Dad stayed on at the factory, doing his part, to be sure.

The war was music and firecrackers, someone else's father far away from home, but not ours. The ration lines were part of it, reinforcing Mom's already considerable frugality. The lines as they formed in the Iowa rain passed a shoemaker's shop and, turning a corner, scaled a flight of cement steps, creating small tents of women and children, moving slowly, talking softly. The shoemaker sat out under his own awning; the smell of his polishes and of the warm leather being scraped and shaped is what comes back to me, and the gluey odor of stiff ration packets at the top of the stairs, pages turning under the pressure of calloused fingers. My mother is efficient, bright—there is adversity in this scene, but it seems too good-natured to be threatening: heavyset bodies under umbrellas, hair under kerchiefs and babushkas, the sounds and smells of good sense, small-town life, the shoemaker's yellow teeth and cordovan-stained fingers, hammering, hammering, his apron a mantle of oxblood and black and India blue. And all of us moving along slowly, slowly, uncomplaining.

Nazis were killing Bohemian gypsies, lining up Jews all across Europe; they stood in lines that moved together slowly, inching forward under dark skies—did Mom and her neighbors think of them? The Europe from where so many of these good midwestern women had come but one generation back was dying in the far distance, but no sound carried this far, into the small ordered community of Lillienthal. These mothers' faces, as steadfast as those of their forebears in Poland and Czechoslovakia and Sweden, were the color of what they would have for dinner: dumplings and chicken gravy, bread pudding and cinnamon tarts, a long way from Krakow and Prague.

The summer before Dennie Lee was born, the four of us took our vacation alongside one of the cool Michigan lakes where friends and business acquaintances of my father kept cabins. We unpacked our new swimming trunks and seersucker shirts on beds tight with khaki blankets, smelled other people's fires in the fireplace, found crumpled shopping lists in the small pantry and wondered who had written them. We read mildewed *National Geographics* by the light of kerosene lamps, retreated to the screened-in porch when lumbering mosquitoes came to call. We swam in lakes with Indian names, dark and deep and still. We looked for arrowheads in the pine forests and at night ate the perch and bass we'd caught that day.

The beaches were thin strips of white sand; creeping through the pine-and-balsam quiet, from sun-dappled clearing to clearing, avoiding the thickets of poison ivy, we'd step out toward another clearing and find it to be the shore of a not-yet-discovered lake, or the southern end of one we'd come upon only from the east. Finding these still, glacial bodies of water was like creating them, and we spent hours crisscrossing the land all around us, eager to chance on each new and sparkling vista.

Occasionally we'd find other bathers, other families there at the water's edge. Brief friendships began and ended in the space of an afternoon. But generally it was the two of us by ourselves, Franklin and me, playing catch, trailing wildlife, endlessly exploring. Exuberantly, now and again, Dad would toss us into the gentle lake— we were just old enough to think it was indecorous of him, but yelped and yelled nonetheless.

It was on one of these pitches that he lost his wedding ring to the lake as well. He realized it only a few minutes afterward, when we'd all dried off and were slumped exhausted on our big itchy plaid blanket. My mother's face was stunned only for a moment, then immediately optimistic; smiling hard, she said she knew we'd find it . . . and we bent to the search, spread out across the sand, moving back and forth on all fours in an extravagant doleful panic each did his best to conceal.

No ring was retrieved that first long afternoon. Nor the afternoon following. We came to the same spot every day, getting a crab's-eye view of life. Endlessly searching and sifting, we were all of us ready to shout out our discovery the next second, or the next . . . or the next. But our vacation came to an end—it was only two weeks, after all—and the ring remained lost to us. The depression at having to return home was compounded by its loss, and we were listless and close-mouthed as we packed the car and prepared to depart.

Then Dad took Franklin back for one last foray; Mom and I sat in our Nash, close to the hamper of hard-boiled eggs and meat-loaf sandwiches we'd packed for the long ride south. And through the curtain of pines and brambles we heard Dad's high ringing tenor, and knew then—as no one had really given up hope—that the ring was found. Mom and I ran to meet them and Dad thrust out his hand with the ring finger again covered; we all basked in the high bright drama of the moment.

We had already been told by Mom, and would be again, by both of them, that their marriage was special, that as soon as they met (and they had, in fact, eloped) they'd known they were meant for each other. The finding of the ring, among those millions and millions of white grains of sand, at the shoreline of the limitless shimmering lake, was an event to conjure with, and conjure with it we two boys did. We sped homeward, two smug children of a blessed union, given allegory that August along with our tans.

I remember the day I shook the hand of Herbert Hoover. It was summer and he had come back to West Branch, Iowa, where he was born. It seemed a ceremony of great pomp, and I was one of the Scouts who helped him with his motorcade. It was a special appearance in honor of his eightieth birthday; he had by then been an ex-president for two decades. Quakers and Amish milled about. He stood on the crest of a hill wearing a white suit, and his cheeks were soft and white, and later he spoke to a sweating crowd. There was no breeze; we boys were all soaked through, but when he shook my hand he was fresh as a baby. I stood amid fields of boys in khaki, in the midst of glory for that long moment, carrying a collapsible flagpole and an acetate flag. What a splendid moment it was. Shaking the hand of celebrity I became celebrity, through some alchemical process I had neither anticipated nor imagined. Like being on TV, and thereby proving one was worthy of being on TV. No equivocations allowed.

Just as we were periodically brought out to see relatives, once or twice a year we were brought down to Dad's office. We felt uncomfortable in both realms, family and business, because we were only decorative objects to be exclaimed over, small soft cushions the grown-ups took care not to sit on. On the beige walls of the office hung calendars from different foundries and suppliers, the largest and most vividly illustrated from a manufacturer of ball bearings: MILES OF SMILES ON TIMKEN BEARINGS emblazoned in a bold hand under each smiling, opulent-hued woman. Beautiful airbrushed faces and shoulders shone beside golden zinnias and red roses, purple asters—

nothing too seductive here: breasts wrapped in tulle and lace and terry cloth, legs and thighs protected by layers and layers of crinolines. Huge and intimidating, because they demanded a response, these goddesses appeared in my preteen dreams, stepping down out of the frame, bending and bowing, about to scoop me up. The calendars I asked to keep, to my father's not-quite-suppressed disappointment, were the ones by Lawson Wood, featuring gangs of orangutans going about their business in a Malaysian community, in hats and coveralls—delicately detailed, drawn and painted in a fairy-tale verisimilitude.

At the office water fountain the men collected and laughed and swore at one another, pounded one another on the shoulder, their shirts rolled up revealing veins like rubber tubing under the skin, the strong smell of pipe and cigar smoke in the air. Outside through the glass was the long industrial sweep of chimneys and warehouses and the plant itself with its burning cauldrons and conveyor belts. The men came and went under clouds of blue smoke, stopping to tousle one's hair, feel one's meager biceps. Dad was alternately jocular and stern with them; I heard the same joke repeated in a half-dozen voices from where I sat, off to the side, with a Lily cup of Coca-Cola balanced on the lip of a stand-up chrome ashtray, a *Field & Stream* magazine open in my lap. When we were very young, the men would pick us up and swing us in the air. As we and they grew older, their behavior became more subdued: they asked us about football or basketball or track, depending on the season, wanted to know what we planned to be when we grew up.

What grown men did was intriguing to think about, but what they actually accomplished in their bustling groups, running back and forth to offices that were surely no larger than my room at home—this was unclear. Something more to it than the jokes and talk about coal and steel and combines, but the secret that made it all so interesting to them had not yet been revealed to me.

Sometimes our father would throw an office party at home. Over their old-fashioneds and Manhattans in the living room the men would grow animated and expansive, almost as hearty as they were beside the water fountain. On these occasions, Mom put out bowls of popcorn and pretzels, trays of cheese and bacon canapés, helped by Mrs Ryan or Mrs Woods, whose husbands were chief among the men. The men's lives were there on their rolled-up sleeves, so open and bold and obtainable, the wives, like Mom, percolating beside them.

Something brazen in all this fellow feeling, something too large for the scale of things.

At Christmas, the good fellowship flowed nonstop—business entertaining became, simply, entertaining: hams and turkeys and boxes of kumquats and grapefruits got delivered and received, presents for wives and children dangled from salesmen's fingers. At parties in our rumpus room, the men of Lillienthal clutched each other's wives to them as they danced the jitterbug and the foxtrot. The women's eyes met over the bouncing sweat-moistened white backs of the men, suffering each festive embrace—glances of sympathy and understanding exchanged over the Ritz crackers and the shrimp; a wrinkling around the eyes as the snowflakes fell outside.

I see it in my mind, Christmas cards taped to the walls and beams of the basement room, and gift poinsettias posed on the bar for maximum effect. I strain to make the scene something more than what it is—though what it is is arguably more than enough. At midnight, champagne corks are popped and couples lean against each other, both soggy and vibrant. The snowflakes are amber, of crystallized bourbon—everyone is somewhat drunk, and the men are topping each other's stories, laughing, singing. Dad's Irish tenor is joined by German and Italian baritones, and in the kitchen Mom's clear sweet voice, a girl's voice really, sings out too, precise about consonants but lax about vowels in the midwestern way; around her the other women share gossip chopped as fine as parsley. It's one of those never-ending scenes that keeps turning, now as then, and we are all of us overwrought and too vivid.

My mother stands by the sink, spoons in her hands, and all the light in the room seems to collect there, in the motion of the dishtowel against them, her short fingers busy, busy as she always was. Once she said to me, "Life is too short to dry silverware," whisking off to some domestic challenge elsewhere—and now, doing just that.

How we change; how we remain the same. I saw my father for the man he was. We got close one night in conversation: I won't let the hair down my back, he said, shaking his head and remembering some youthful indiscretion, but I understand, I understand. And I think he did, though we never much talked of it again. He understood the flesh. I sometimes think our family was all flesh: my mother young and triumphant on the Lion's Club float, parading through dry leaves and low whistles; Dad a burst of Irish muscle, crashing through the lines at Maquoketa College.

Childhood. That time of one's life when nothing goes

out and everything comes in—when circumstances are the only facts. Children that are part of life, but not yet part of living, seeing every act as a rehearsal for some later performance. It's a bright agony we all endure, but who knew it at the time? Then, it seemed something close to bliss.

One of the things about being raised in a family of boys is that you're pulled into a tumult of sporting endeavors, whether or not you have the talent or inclination. The ball is thrown; you must raise your hands and catch it. In the beginning, it may not always be so simple, or so easy, but the sporting life has a way of wearing you down.

Our elementary school was a big brick building in the middle of dusty playing fields, in a section of town that was neither downtown or uptown, with a drugstore across the street and a grocery store to one side. In the spring of the year, we all played softball and volleyball on those patchwork fields, avoiding puddles, and kicking dandelions and playing tag between games, responding with varying interest to the sport at hand.

My fourth-grade teacher, Mr Sweeney, had brought us all out to the diamond one morning for physical education. Out in left field, where little was required of me, I was not unhappy thinking my own unsporting thoughts, far away from whatever was happening around that sacred patch of earth and rosin, home plate. The Iowa sun was already steamy above us, the gardens opposite the fields redolent with lilacs and forsythia. Nothing could have been further from my mind than the small white object which suddenly appeared in the sky above me, soundlessly, as if from another universe. It had, alas, come straight from the bat of Donnie Farley, and it found me splayfooted and stiff-armed, in an attitude Mr Sweeney loudly declared that of a goldarned sun worshiper. Later, as we walked back toward the building, I was seared by the scorn. The fact that Mr Sweeney looked amazingly like Robert Mitchum, and that I had something of a crush on him, made the situation worse.

That afternoon at recess I was found looking up the skirts of the girls who swung across the monkey bars, and was pulled into the principal's office by the ear. What sort of young man *was* I, old bewigged Mrs Leander wanted to know. That, of course, was the question on my mind as well. I wept, I think, at the uncertainty of my position: was I a sissy (sun worshiper) or was I a dirty little boy like all the rest of them? And which was it better to be? Sexual confusion crept in at an early age, apparently, as it not uncommonly does. I found sports and sex to be two strands of the same fiber; proving oneself for others was the function of both. But this came later; for the moment, sex was an event occurring elsewhere—all I really felt was that what was expected of one in this life was far more complicated than it had appeared to be. And, occasionally, far more painful to determine.

The boy whose bat it was that prompted this lesson, Donnie Farley, was a recurring terror in my young life.

Donnie's father was a sporting celebrity, in Lillienthal at least, having been awarded the Mr Iowa (Eastern Division) trophy for bodybuilding two times, with a third title gleaming in the not unforeseeable future. Toward that end, and others not specified, Drew Farley pumped up his enormous biceps and preternaturally wide pectorals, during warm weather, on a jerry-built balcony that jutted out over his green-shingled house on Maiden Lane, behind the woods next to Tillie Wagoner's garden, but still visible in the distance from our own front steps. To Franklin and me, he resembled one of those frogs we pursued out on Five Mile Road, pale and bloated, stuck like a specimen from biology class on the flat slide of his own roof. In clothes or out of them, he was oily and too smug by half, and the yeast pills he took gave him bad breath as well.

To have such a father can't have been easy. Donnie and I were the same age, civil but never chummy from kindergarten on up; it was in the fourth grade that we began to fight. It started in a random way, as if he'd had to fight someone, and he guessed it might as well be me. I had no experience, had only run in once or twice when Franklin was on top of someone in the schoolyard and given the underdog a quick smack. Mainly, mine was a placid personality.

Donnie would wait for me on the way home, in a vacant lot off Bellevue Avenue, and inevitably spectators would appear, from our own school, and from Lady of Lourdes down the hill. I had a friend named Ray Woolley, who was tough and freckled and red-haired, and whose father worked at my father's plant as a truck driver. He thought it was dumb of me to fight, if I didn't

19

want to—who's pushing you? he wanted to know. We walked slowly toward the lot, and I knew I couldn't just pretend Donnie wasn't there and walk away from it the way Ray urged me to. Nobody could really call Donnie a bully, because I was taller, and probably (certainly) weighed more than he. No, I had to fight because that was what was expected.

Donnie was lean and sharp-featured, and spoke no more than was necessary. He stepped forward as I arrived. Then came the long moment of putting down my books and putting up my fists. We circled each other in what seemed the correct preliminary mode, a little closer each time, with the Lourdes riffraff urging us on. If by chance I landed the first punch, my advantage was soon turned against me—this was to be an exhibition bout for Donnie, not a real contest, that was understood, and if I got above myself, as sparring partner and punching bag, he glared at me as if I'd insulted the whole process. Shortly we'd be on the ground, wrestling in the dust, and maybe I'd get something in my eye and have to quit, or stay doubled over long enough from a gut punch that it would all come to an end. The worst days were when it wouldn't come to an end, but went on and on, when there seemed to be no reason or passion in the fighting, nothing but circumstance to justify the tyranny. Walking toward that empty lot was like walking out toward the end of the high diving board at the YMCA: I knew absolutely and forever that I couldn't possibly go through it again, but the body that carried these protests kept moving, and there I was.

All one spring we fought, and I wonder if he thought of it as some kind of training, as if such tussles were his due.

When summer came, his enmity abruptly ceased—it had to do with school, and after school, I guess. It certainly didn't have to do with me.

❖

I wanted to make people smile, not glower. I wanted to have an effect on others, but I shrank from enforcing my will. I wanted to decorate my life. On Saturday afternoons in fifth and sixth grade, I took the bus to the local art museum and spent three hours engaged in pastel drawing. On the first floor the museum had a number of small nineteenth-century paintings hung in a long dark curtained gallery—some from the Hudson River School, along with midwestern scenes of considerably less ambition. Against the walls of thick painted brocade, the paintings were spaced like windows. A dusty museum smell was in the air, something foreign and herbal, and I always felt quite subdued by the heavy decorum of the place. A somber guard prowled the premises, scowling at laughter or too rapid progress from canvas to canvas.

Upstairs, it was all chalk dust and light, and the steady hum of creative activity as twenty intense young artists pored over fountains and horses and woodland scenes, smudging their pinks and greens and umbers "for effect." The instructor, a stout woman in a flowing smock and with a mane of aqua hair, passed like a good fairy from one drawing board to another, her stick of Conté a wand, serenely imparting not a drop of wisdom but gallons of praise: smiling, indiscriminate. A potter's wheel turned in an adjoining room, and we witnessed transfixed the serpentine coiling of a pot as it was spun and smoothed into shape, the potter's foot pumping steadily, hypnotically. The smell of wet clay combined with the dry sweet fragrance of the chalk, producing a heady earnest perfume.

Chicago was a four-hour drive from Lillienthal, a trip made over the slowly churning Mississippi, then through fields and small towns, finally between the stacks of brick and tar paper and wood that were the dwellings of the western suburbs. Chicago was the pungent smell of the stockyards, like the stink of boiled shoes, and the clouds of soot and smoke along the tracks of the El. And, most vividly, it was the Art Institute.

On twice-a-year class trips, I'd stand before the glistening Gauguins as before saints on an altar, wondering at the burning power of *The Spirit of the Dead Watches* and *The Spring of Delight*. They were holy pieces, and I revered them. Moving through the rooms of Impressionists, admiring the pastel fury of Degas, the limpid power of Monet, I was oblivious to the snickering of my friends, the cute asides occasioned by a confrontation with great works of art. I was transported, in those rooms—the plane of art was the only plane worth aspiring to, clearly; the fellowship of painters was the only community for me. I was eager to pledge myself to Art, if only Art would have me. It was easy to think of myself living an artist's life, which apparently had to do mainly with behaving extravagantly and dying young, and I scurried over the marble floors of the Art Institute imagining myself as one with the creators of all I beheld.

The nimbus of empathy and intention lasted for a period of days, back in Lillienthal—days that tumbled down on one another, finally ended in a heap. With my drawing pad open before me, back in my room, I came to rest in a jumble of frustration and self-disgust, faced with my bountiful inadequacy. If I could only concentrate on the life, and not the work itself, it might be easier. The painter's life was sure to combine art and praise, sex and celebrity, in a seamless luminous blend . . . one would dwell among voluptuous savages. Abandoning quotidian restraints, the painter, like his paintings, would inspire adulation and love. It was a lovely mantle to wrap around oneself, splashed with Gauguin's dark faces and bright flowers.

However much I was encouraged in my creative pursuits, I was never unaware of my parents' expectations for me, as regarded self-sufficiency, as regarded making a living. Domestic upper-middle-class life was where we were all bound, my brothers and I; we were raised to be family men. Dad was attentive to the details of our development, liberal in the way of one who had climbed up out of the Depression and made a successful life. He wanted us all to have the opportunity to make choices, but to be able to provide for our own progeny when the time came. Self-sufficiency was what we were being prepared for— roused out of bed on frosty mornings to deliver newspapers, sent across the river to work at Hamilton Beach.

We all worked at what we could get, as other children did: topping onions in the field, picking raspberries, shucking corn, selling doughnuts and potholders and magazine subscriptions door to door. I mowed the lawn all one summer on the grounds of the Masonic Temple and Home, washed the windows of the old folks' rooms there, sang songs I thought they'd like from my ladder-perch, was rebuffed by ancient cold shoulders. I worked at the Kinney Shoe Store, wedging flat working-class feet into summer pumps, squeezing the tiny pastrylike toes of infants into their first white leather boxes. Along with my brothers, I was taught to be industrious, and the newspapers we all tossed onto stoops and porches over the years, circumventing dogs and sprinklers, were a small forest's worth.

The job I held the longest, longer than delivering papers or selling shoes, or peddling Spud-nuts door to door, was that of caddy at the River Hills Country Club.

Lying on the bank of the river, toes stuck in the dark sandy mud and head back against the cane and willow, I was an extremely happy fifteen. The water of the Mississippi lapped at my daydreams, and the sounds of the other caddies, as they hollered and swung from a tire that hung from a craggy sycamore, were like waves and eddies that traveled west with its flow. The great muddy river, otherwise describing a long north-south meridian through the body of the midwest, at Lillienthal turned in its direction, and provided the meandering profile with a nose, under which we now frolicked. Here the river was warm.

It was always a hot sticky summer in Iowa, and on the long afternoons, the golfers at the country club were disinclined toward competition in the noonday hours. They sat, their faces red, their calves bloated, fanning themselves over gin and tonics in the club's upstairs lounge. A black man, Horace, who had been at the club for generations, brought them towels and replenished glasses, cool and efficient through the languorous days—these were mainly white-haired gentlemen who knew when to take their ease, sprawled about on benches and wicker chairs, perspiring judiciously into thick white towels passed out by Horace as a well-oiled Bombay fan turned overhead. They told professional stories—they were lawyers and doctors and men in real estate—and smoked very good cigars.

Out on the golf course, the greens were turning brown, on their way to an August the color of wheat. Beside the green of the eighteenth hole, the club pro sweated in the shade of a willow, while before him Mrs Timmerman and then Mrs Lewis and finally Mrs Donovan thrashed at the grass.

A caddy was a kind of servant, and though "patronize" was not a word I then knew, it was an idea I felt. It hovered around these tan wives, the spouses of the men in the lounge, almost audible in their long self-assured strides, their clever caps and plaid skirts, the discreet flapping of the fringed tongues of their powdered shoes as they crossed mile after mile of grassland. Women intent on themselves and the appearance of their lives. Women who had gained their lives of leisure at some cost, and *would* enjoy themselves.

With the husbands, it was more relaxed—they and I could be chums of a sort for eighteen holes, chums while I washed their Dunlaps and Spaldings, and they bought me a Dr. Pepper on the tenth hole, chums because I played golf too, and what mattered about the game, to them, had nothing to do with my carrying their bags, or even helping them line up a putt.

The caddies saw through them all, cracked wise and philosophical.

The boys smoked cigarettes and played strip poker in the caddy shack on rainy days; the older caddies told stories to the younger boys, and cursed the weather and sent their subordinates to the main building to buy Pepsi-Cola and hot dogs. The shack stank like a latrine on wet afternoons; under the corner where a toilet had been cut in the floor, rainwater collected in puddles. There were steps made of long planks which you walked up to enter the building, itself built on stilts; the wood smelled of years of boys and dampness.

Drawings were scratched on the wall, fitted to the knot-holes, and torn yellowing comics lay under the benches. No one ever read books. The other caddies were from schools other than mine, other towns—were farmboys and boys from across the river, from the factory towns. They had long hair, often curly, and sideburns once they had whiskers. Their names were Dallas and Skeeter and Fletcher, and there were a number of Rays.

Skinny-dipping in the river was one of the best parts of the job during the hot summer months; whenever the caddy master came out and let us know we could beat it for a while, we did, straight down to the muddy water. One afternoon, a little upriver from where we usually swam, Franklin and I and some of his friends—I was usually the youngest—came across a boy of nine or ten, truculent and dirty, who was pushing young puppies into the current. He was making temporary rafts for each of the animals—temporary because once they got out into the swiftly moving water, they went under. This was his intention; he lived nearby and had been told by his parents to drown the litter or he'd have to get rid of the female who'd produced them.

Three were left when we arrived, and they were greasy pathetic little mutts. We grabbed one, and two of our companions did the same. We chased the boy back into the canebreak and proceeded down to our usual secluded spot, assuring each other that no parent of ours could turn away such a small and unassuming item, most especially when they'd heard the circumstances of their acquisition. We built a pen of limbs and sticks for them next to a weather-beaten log; while the other boys splashed and pushed each other under the water, one of us kept watch over the tender band.

Half a dozen of us were there that day. One was Lionel, who had only one testicle, and another was long sly Jeffrey, whom I had always regarded as something of a cold fish—but who had taken the dog and cradled it, in a show of unexpected warmth. We couldn't go back to the caddy yard with the dogs, so we guessed caddying was over for the day. Hitchhiking back into Lillienthal, with the puppies stuck in our shirts, wouldn't be a problem.

Skeeter and Dallas came down after a while—they usually hung around together—bringing a six-pack of beer with them. They made fun of us for saving the dogs and threatened to toss them into the water if we didn't watch out, and then came the usual scuffling, and us swiping beers, and bumming a drag on their cigarettes. The day wore itself out, and we were all lying on the riverbank, and then Skeeter suggested we have a circle jerk, and that's what we did.

Seeing who could shoot the farthest was the point; we were all of us naked anyway. It did not seem odd to be thus engaged with one's brother—though I was curious about the similarities in our equipment. We squinted our eyes and pumped away. Every so often one of the guys would call out the name of a girl at school; it sailed up like a clay pigeon over our weaponry. Skeeter and Dallas jerked each other off, but none of the rest of us exchanged the favor. Since it had to be a contest, there had to be a winner, and it was Jeffrey, who got the last can of beer as his prize. We all dove into the water, and washed off, then gathered up our sleeping puppies and made our way home.

Elation followed me back; Franklin and I were able to convince Mom without much effort that the puppy was meant to be ours, and we went to bed feeling we had done something humane and benevolent. Sleep rolled over me like the warm river, Skeeter and Dallas floating for an instant before my eyes, just before the dark.

During those same summer months as we got our dog, Toby, I became reacquainted with a girl who had been my dancing partner when we were both brought to the Outing Club, by our parents, to learn the two-step and the waltz. I was sitting with the other caddies, discussing the athletic merits of the Clinton River Rats and the Muscatine Blue Devils, playing splits, and hoping for a double-eighteen with a big tip at the end.

Sammy—Samantha—strode back and forth across the practice green, lining up putts, looking cool and mature in lime-green shorts and blouse and white visor over her blond hair. She recognized me first—she had changed and I hadn't, I suppose, still something of an urchin squatting with the other boys—and said my name. I went over to where she stood on the green, although we weren't supposed to, and made small talk while I retrieved the balls she sent slowly skimming across the wet turf. She liked the idea I was a caddy—it had more heft than dancing partner—and I liked the way she shook her hair, and the way she let herself show when she was interested in something. At fifteen we were all cooler-than-thou. So Sammy and I started up, and it became the main affair of my teenage life, if a relationship never quite consummated but always on the brink, a relationship long on romance and short on intromission, can properly be called an affair.

She lived across the road from the club, and her parents were rather elegant; her father and my father had been friends at Maquoketa College, and our families were not displeased when we started seeing each other.

Her father had his own Piper Cub, and as he was leaving the club one afternoon he asked me if I'd like to come along for a ride. Hy Henson, the pro who instructed Mrs Lewis and Mrs Timmerman, heard the invitation, and I saw him having a word with Sammy's father while he changed from his spikes to his street shoes next to the pro shop. Mr Burris said, loud enough to hear, that he supposed he knew who was all right and who wasn't, thank you. I know that old Henson looked on me with greater suspicion after that—he didn't like it when members' sons wanted to caddy, and he certainly didn't like it when caddies got too familiar with the members.

Mr Burris took me for the ride, and let me pull the stick that sent us nosing downward, then upward through the thin cloudless air. I was queasy, but hadn't embarrassed myself by the time we landed. The *order* of the cornfields and riverine tributaries around Lillienthal was what impressed me, as if behind all the makeshift construction and planting was a plan everyone had agreed on and implemented. We flew low over the club, and a few figures reached up and waved their tiny tam-o'-shanters; we saw it for what it was, an irregular tract of yellow-green, dotted with sand traps that looked as if they had been painted in, little red flags on circles of brighter green, all of it wispy and insubstantial. The fields around it, of onions and corn and soybeans, were green turning blue; the vestigial woods seemed nearly black against the relentless green flatness. As we floated down, the green came up to meet us and took shape and substance, and our outing was over. Later, Sammy told me her father liked the way I was quiet and didn't jabber.

Her mother can hardly have had the same impression. If I was reticent with men, with women I was garrulous, unconstrained. Sammy and I talked of all our future plans, our theories of life and art. She was bound to be an actress, and the two of us fed our plans into the gleaming hopper of anticipated success, unreservedly, neither realizing that such success would take us in different directions, pull us apart. For we both wanted To Live. The summer of *West Side Story* we sang "Tonight" and "Maria" at the top of our lungs along the club's fairways at dusk, startling the groundskeepers and the starlings. We would go to the Coliseum Ballroom and dance and dance— perhaps we used each other as props, perhaps what we really loved was the way we looked on the dance floor, huffing and puffing toward delirium, certifiably happy together, under the spotlights.

We lay down on the same fairways we sang along, and drank in the moonlight and the summer and the sounds of Zola Taylor and the Platters that drifted out from the bar. During dances at River Hills we jitterbugged on the tennis courts, unnetted for the evening, and poured stolen whiskey into our punch. We swam in the pool, and I hardly did any caddying at all. I was smug, as tan as Sammy; every once in a while I'd feel Henson's narrowed eye on me, and sensing his disapproval would enjoy myself all the more.

At the Caddy Banquet in September, when sets of woods and irons were given out to the boys who had excelled in the Monday (caddies day) tournaments, or had been the most punctual or the most helpful, I was given a set of Cary Middlecoff irons for being—this brought a round of catcalls and hisses as I moved up through the crowd of boys to accept my prize—the Best-Looking Caddy. Henson had in this "award" thought to give me something of a comeuppance, but I was oblivious to the intended slur, if slur it was.

The old pro notwithstanding, I think people generally wished Sammy and me well. My parents did; her parents did. She was beautifully formed, thin-waisted; her sweet breasts and hips rubbed against me on the dance floor,

31

and her hair smelled of lilies of the valley. She ought to have been enough for any young man. For the years we were coming to ourselves we gave each other a kind of picture-book joy, and trusted each other and grabbed hold of each other's bodies, knowing we were entitled. Although that knowledge left me when other knowledge came to bear, in my young adolescence I was more than content with what I had.

Franklin and I, when we were Cub Scouts dressed in blue and yellow, and then Boy Scouts in khaki and red, were encouraged to compete with the other boys in various fields of expertise and knowledge, and we were expected to excel. Franklin made it to a higher rank than I; I managed First Class, earned two merit badges, and then stopped. Around me, boys went on to Life and Eagle, appearing at Scout functions in long serapes of merit badges, able to spout litanies of trees and wildflowers, to pull together bowlines and sheepshanks with careless ease, succeed again and again.

At Boy Scout camp—as distinguished from jamboree and camporee, briefer endeavors—we lived in cabins, but in other seasons we slept in sleeping bags, lying flat on top of the Iowa soil next to the smoldering fire, then under the root-smelling canvas flaps. The mosquitoes came in and poked at us; occasionally we poked at each other. Wet layers of kapok rustled here and there, punctuated by snorts and giggles, mock snoring. From pine boughs horned owls looked down, watching through the night. At dawn we shivered and shook out the damp covers, ignored whomever we'd slept pressed against.

Scout behavior was codified; the law of the troop was something we memorized and recited at meetings. We were first of all supposed to be Trustworthy. That meant keeping our mouths shut; it was what you didn't say that was important. There was also Loyalty, which wasn't at all hard to embody.

Loyalty was friendship and nobility and schoolboy crushes: I was loyal to various older boys who never knew it. One of these, a swimming instructor at the YMCA, also gave the troop lifesaving instruction. His name was John Kloss, and he was blond and strong-jawed, with a swimmer's shoulders and thighs. We all stayed under water as long as we could to please him, stepped off the diving board amid the echoing shouts of our fellow Tadpoles and Minnows, swallowed mouthfuls of tepid chlorinated water in our efforts to succeed. He crouched naked at the edge of the pool—it was before swimming trunks were worn at the Y—and we pummeled the water, inching toward him, our shriveled little selves so visibly inferior to his dangling adulthood that we might have been another species entirely. Those who splashed the most valiantly were rewarded by his laughter, his good-natured shove back into the pool, the slap of his hand on their bare bottoms, just before the plunge.

The boyness of Boy Scouting is what signified: a bond squared that would later be cubed. Scouting blended family and friendship, sports and life, for after Mr Vito, the scoutmaster, resigned, my father took over the small

33

neighborhood troop. Franklin and I then had a double role model leading us through the woods, reading out the different characteristics of pin oaks and maples. When we reached high school he was elected to the school board, going to meetings with the other board members. The board's decisions drifted back to us, and we felt a connection with power, as a school board touches the power of any small town. Dad got larger and larger as we grew older.

Coaches often came to the house during junior high and high school. Dad had been on the football and track teams in college, and was still a sportsman (golf, fishing, deer hunting). We'd sometimes see him standing on the sidelines at football practice—his presence had on me not so much a reinforcing as an inhibiting effect. Franklin didn't mind.

What is it we were taught out there on the football field? The coaches stood barking instructions, the boys curled and uncurled like crustaceans in their padded shells. All of us striving so, urging each other on. A barrage of insults repeated day after day was an integral part of it all—the barrage is what remains, not the glory of winning, or the good-fellowship.

The worst thing the coach could call you was a girl. If it was Coach Jenkins, his face would collect in a red balloon of rage, and the spittle would fly; his always bloodshot eyes would narrow and he would pull the leather cap from his head, fling it to the ground. He'd send someone running under a rain of epithets toward the track, for his stupidity, or timidity, or both. Coach Jenkins and his wife, Penny, sometimes came to our house on the weekend, sat with a drink in our living room, rehashing victory or defeat. Dad could never get over the fact that Penny Jenkins used coarse language. "A lady never says 'shit,' " said he. But whatever Coach had to say was all right.

❖

Boy Scouts and ladylike phrases: we were born in a time when and a place where men's and women's lore was divided up, kept separate. A small town in the midwest before the time of shopping centers, a tribe continually shushing itself. A people scurrying to make do, to keep things in order, perpetuate itself.

High school teachers appear in quick attitudes, like pink stars stuck on a gray '50s flag—Mr Adams, the vice-principal, bearish and devout, discovered in the back row of the Carleton Cinema where he'd come to see the forbidden Brigitte Bardot slowly unwinding herself from a sheet in *And God Created Woman*; Mr Wingate, the geometry teacher, sweet and goggle-eyed, waving his pep-club pennant, cheering on the team; Miss Bundrage, the girls' gym teacher, gangly and demure, applying her lipstick while holding court on the bleacher seats between classes; Mr Ingram, bald and flatulent, puffing through chorus; finally, Mr Arletty of American history, sweat-stained to his waist in all seasons, running to the window at the sound of a fire engine, leaning out, abandoning Taft and tariffs and Boss Tweed.

Families came in tiers, brothers and cousins standing upon one another's shoulders—the football team and wrestling team had Shusters and Laymans and Witters for decades. These were big rangy boys, with hands like shovels and smiles that would melt butter. Once in a while a boy would appear in school with a black eye or a scraped jaw, with the story that there had been a brotherly row, fists thrown among the haystacks, serious scrapping in the barn. The Cairn brothers, Dan and Don, who usually proceeded with perfect smart-ass felicity regarding each other, occasionally had to be held apart in wood-working—a sudden murderous intensity in their eyes and fists would overtake them and then they would have at each other without a word.

But generally the farmboys were relaxed, easygoing. Their hands smelled like manure in the morning, foot-ball and rosin after three o'clock. They pulled at the pink pointed blouses of the sophomore and junior girls, exchanged eight-page bibles at lunch, flipped through their pages, got a hard-on and a laugh, slept through civics. They hung out, too, with the bad boys from the trailer camps who had cousins across the river; they were second- and third-generation German and Irish families plowing the hard soil, bowlegged from tractors and horses. They sped across the river, where it was only eighteen to drink, got drunk in their backseats, and drag-raced back across the bridge. Raised hell all weekend, were men at puberty: catapulted through their young lives like the cowboys their daddies had all wanted to be and almost were, but got stuck too far east for that; han-dled midwestern Holsteins instead of western Appa-loosas; bounced along and never looked down, wanted life just to get past beneath them. Age gathered early across their foreheads, and those of their young wives, like rocks in the soil—they had children dripping from their loins when they were still children themselves, inflating their gingham bellies, forcing them to leave school early. They had appetites precipitate and sly, were only heard of, never seen, populated wheat and soybean galaxies, distant and doomed.

One Christmas we heard about a crash early in the morning: two Muscatine boys and one of our own, coming home, skidding on the highway, dead before they sobered up. Our boy was Rich Swayze, curly-haired and sixteen. We all went to his funeral, and stopped at his farm afterward. Trucks and cars from all over were pulled up against the barn, parked along the road; his mother thin-lipped and dry-eyed between her older sons; her baby boy gone to hell with bad companions. He was a wrestler, two weights below me, coming up, stepping into life. Sailing along. It was an odd thing, how much his death touched us all.

Millard Hughes used to come to school with his toenails painted. Red and chipped, shining like little shells at the bottom of his big-boned country frame. Nobody ever asked him why; big and tough, he did what he liked. It was Millard and his friend Joey Pinto who found poor Betsy Fiddler's body one morning on their way to school, close by Devil's Glen Trailer Park, stuffed in the bushes next to the bridge across the little river there. The killer was never apprehended, and Millard and Pinto shut up about it after the first two or three days. It was like a sudden explosion, a burst of random violence in a town where nothing seemed random. The white body found lying beside the black asphalt road, the photograph in the newspaper, then nothing. Someone passing through, someone from down by the railroad tracks, a friend?

Not too many mysteries in our small town. The mysteries would occur to us all later, when we had grown up and moved away. Our curiosity was about the future; the present was a closed book. Familiar people who acted strangely were still . . . familiar.

We liked the men who were tough and callous, men with tattoos winding up their arms. We were all going to be tough. One autumn, Franklin and I went with Gerald Page and his cousin Eddie out to the carnival at the county fairgrounds. The rides along the midway were spectacular; Gerald and Eddie smoked Camels as they strode along. We rode the Ferris wheel and the Tilt-a-Whirl and got sick, and recovered, and won kewpie dolls on silver canes at the shooting gallery.

The Page boys had an uncle who had been a juggler on the midway and who'd told them to say "I'm with it" to the barkers so they'd know not to hustle them. "I'm with it" meant you'd worked at carnivals and weren't just another rube. We tried it out, swaggering through the sawdust, hands deep in our pockets, looking tough. The man with all the stuffed animals abruptly stopped his spiel and flashed us a grin; the woman with yellowish skin at the bingo tent gave us a nod. We went into the sideshow tents, enthralled by the woman suspended in a vat of green water, the hairy "wolf child," the hermaphrodite wearing half a man's costume, half a woman's. Overconfident, we snuck through the back flap of the adults-only tent and crawled around behind the stage. A big nasty redhead moved around under a blue spotlight; beetles and river moths hit the light with a snapping sound, one after the other, in a kind of Morse code, and there was the sound of the rough men calling up to her and her yelling back. She moved to music from a record that had crowd noises on it, scratchy and overinflated, like something heard echoing from a distance. When we edged around to the front, we saw that she was stalking back and forth across the wooden stage, now and again crouching down at its edge. Every time she crouched, the men would cheer and whistle, and then we saw that she was picking up silver dollars the men placed on end there.

Her eyes were painted black and her hair was a taffy-apple red, and she wore black feathers in it; her breasts were white, scarlet at the nipples, and there was a kind of grass skirt tied at her waist. As she bobbed upright, her eyes scanned the dark enclosure, and she thrust out her tongue. Suddenly she caught sight of us, and pointed a long menacing finger. "Hey, you gents! What the hell are *you* doing in here?" she demanded. A few heads turned to look; she stood high above us and laughed, then again dropped down to the floor. We stood open-mouthed, then a big Hispanic man came after us, swearing and spitting, and we ran out through the exit flap and got away. We'd seen more than we bargained for. Eddie and Franklin said it was really cool, but I was deeply offended, came home and was sick again, didn't want to think about it.

My sexual education was patched together from such

bright pieces. Sex, of course, was one of the main mysteries. I had learned from Franklin, earlier, that the way people made babies was for the man to pee in the woman when she wasn't looking. He had got this information from Danny Sujek down the block; Danny was already in high school at this point, and his opinion and store of knowledge counted for a lot. But the image was not what one had in mind. Incredulous, finally crestfallen, I had trouble looking Mom in the eye for a time.

Dad, getting wind of our misinformation, took Franklin and me out among the backyard four-o'clocks and disabused us of the toilet notion, illustrating with stamens and sepals what the process of fertilization was all about. The nonurinary function of our own equipment was explained to us, briskly and efficiently. Dad let us know that aggression was the key, that in sexual matters we were to take what we wanted without asking for a by-your-leave from our partners. Lust was acknowledged by all to be a relentless thing for the male—Sammy once asked me if it was true that the man, once he got started, couldn't stop. Telling her the truth, I felt myself traitorous, at odds with the prevailing winds of adolescence. Sexual arrogance was the habit we boys were to put on.

I never got it right, was something of a washout in the perseverance department. Tears (from Karla, or Candi, or Dora Mae) had on me an instant anti-aphrodisiac effect. I never arrived at that place where nothing mattered but getting it up and getting it in. "Never up, never in!" the golfers used to say to each other, with a wink, on the River Hills greens.

The girls in our high school were subdued about their own sexuality, and all one's gumption was needed to overcome their inertia. But one classmate of mine was rather less refined. In study hall and geography class, I used to receive notes from Roxanne Brewer that said simply, "Eat me." Square-shaped and sporting an auburn DA, Roxanne smiled her foxy smile at me across the pages of blue maps and yellowing desktops, slowly twisting the points of her upturned Judy Garland collar. I found her terrifying, never took a bite.

Sammy and I as a couple didn't make it through our senior year together. Just before school started up that August, she was spending a lot of time around the club swimming pool. I found that the reason was a member's son named Tom, a diver on vacation from Choate: blond and heavy-limbed and intent on having his way with her. (I ought to have known her question re male momentum wasn't strictly academic.) He had it, finally, and to say I shrank from competition thereafter would be cruelly correct. Who knows if we would have stayed together, in our lustful if innocent state, if it hadn't been for rude, unflagging Tom. At any rate, the world was getting larger for us both that season.

In August, on the Mississippi, the mud of the riverbanks would cake and split apart and peel up at the corners like the irregular sections of an old jigsaw puzzle. The smell of the river, and the smaller streams that led into it, was stale, and the flies and gnats and dragonflies hovering over the brown water's surface would give the impression of movement where none occurred. It was as if the river stopped flowing in August, and only sat there. Near the town of Muscatine were enormous sand dunes and mined-out quarries where couples would drive to spend an afternoon or evening. It was a long drive from Lillienthal, because it was hot, and the land was flat, with miles of cattails and reeds on one side of the road and withered grassland on the other. By the time you got to the dunes, you'd be so parched you'd splash down into the water right away, tempted to drink from the still pools instead of merely submerging yourself.

I came there when I was seventeen, three August Saturdays in a row, with a student from the Palmer School of Chiropractic, who worked part-time as a bellboy at the Blackhawk Hotel. He had a room up above the pickles and beets and sliced roast beef of the smorgasbord; I stopped there for a cool drink after meeting him in the record department of Whitfield's Department Store the first Saturday. He had slick hair and soft eyes, and he showed me photographs of a summer he'd been to Greece.

I knew we were going to do something, but I didn't know quite what it was, and when he asked if I'd like to drive down to the quarries with him, I remember I didn't hesitate for a second before saying yes. My parents thought I was hot-rodding around with some of the other guys from school, speeding along in somebody's raked and customized, turned-down and glass-packed pride-and-joy. But I was on my own, with a 45 single of Jackie Wilson's "Reet Petite" clutched under my arm and someone who'd been to Greece stepping on the gas beside me. We got to the dunes and out of our clothes—though we both kept on our jockey shorts—and were down into the water in nothing flat.

He produced a half-empty bottle of sloe gin from his glove compartment, and I loved the sticky sweet taste of it. No one was anywhere near where we had parked the car—the beauty of the quarries was that with so many small coves and pools, it had the feel of a very private place. I've learned since that while we slowly approached each other above the surface, beneath us there was occurring even more rarefied sexual activity—the gestation of a species of mud turtle known nowhere else in the country or the world but in that sandy quarry. To think of it, then, I would have thought the Muscatine turtles to be as common as the mud on which Bayard and I lay. One's own singularity was all that mattered.

Before it got dark, and after we had taken off our cotton shorts and got ahold of each other, and spent ourselves in the water and on the sand and finally in the front seat of that old gin-smelling DeSoto, we drove back through the cattail marshes and fields of corn, to Lillienthal. I went on to where I was expected—a session of preseason weight training for the football team.

That first night after Bayard I felt something magical had occurred. I was a dynamo of prowess, filled with a rare strength, able to outshine the other guards and halfbacks. Exotic nights flashed before my eyes as I went through the exercises. Something like a moral invincibility cloaked me. The power of an undiscovered life—a truly adult way of being—came over me, and I outmuscled the rest of the team to set the evening's record in push-ups, sit-ups, and leg raises.

Afterward, at home in my bedroom, I didn't sleep. The

adrenaline that had been unleashed in me kept barking through my veins. This body I had, this thing that had been lacking its own authority for so long, had suddenly come together, and hardened to a purpose I recognized as natural and just, no matter how outlandish it might seem to others. The secretness of it was part of it—I had never, as far as I could remember, been admonished *against* making love to a man. The subject hadn't come up.

The potency of unspoken sexuality filled the night around me that August. I stayed mum, and went on with my seventeenth year. But over my old life, a new life had formed.

In February of my last year of high school in Lillienthal, I came home from wrestling practice, went straight to my father's liquor cabinet, and finished off half a bottle of Old Crow. I was alone and got drunk and headed for New Orleans. Liquor was fuel for my impulse, and it kept me warm through the wet afternoon and evening.

I recall I started out down by the railway tracks, imagining I'd be able to find a boxcar headed south. Prowling among the ice-encrusted railway cars, I soon realized they were locked in for the night, if not the season. The local freight train I'd heard all my life didn't make a full stop in Lillienthal, as I'd always imagined—it slowed but continued its rattling journey at a nonnegotiable clip, and, running along beside it, I cursed its speed and heedless girth. I had to leave town, would leave town, though I couldn't then say why. The whiskey kept me chuckling to myself as I trudged along the tracks. It was warm in New Orleans, wasn't it?—and that was reason enough.

I was going to New Orleans, and the river would take me there. Down on the levee at night, men who worked on the paddle wheelers, or who were passing through, heading downriver to Memphis and the Gulf, would congregate. When we were younger, Mom and Dad had taken Franklin and me for walks along the levee, holding us up so we could look out over the loading of boats, the movements of winches and barges. Old Don Hammer sometimes worked on the levee, and when I was delivering newspapers he'd tell me about the accidents he'd seen—a man hit by a falling bale and paralyzed for life, a novice struck with a baling hook, a captain knocked overboard and nearly swept away. His accounts were gleeful, filled with the blood and thunder of a catch-as-catch-can life.

The levee in winter was bleak. Truck drivers collected around a drum fire: half a dozen men with dark faces, walking up and down, stretching their legs before they crossed the bridge and took the highway south through Illinois, down into Missouri, finally Arkansas, Louisiana. The river was open, and a barge was drawn up at the end of the loading pier—how long it had been moored there was hard to tell. Next to it lay the *River Queen*, and as I moved closer I could see light in its cabins and men moving along the passageways and decks. The *River Queen* churned up and down the Mississippi during the summer months. Once I'd gone for a ride on it with my girlfriend, Sammy. A band had been playing, and it was great fun slipping and sliding on the dance floor as the current changed and the band changed with it. But I'd never thought about where it went or what it did during the winter when no pleasure-seekers queued up at the dock, no wedding parties waited to be carried away.

It must have been about nine o'clock at night now, and the damp winter rain was beginning to put a chill in my traveling plans. Steam rose up from the water, or a kind of fog. Laughter came from on board, and the smell of soup and cigarettes drifted out of the portholes.

I stood on the dock, watching the mysterious motions of the figures in the dark as they passed back and forth over the lighter surface of the paddle wheeler. Cigarettes lighted up like fireflies; lengths of white rope were tossed here and there.

The door of the cabin nearest the gangplank burst open then, and out of the swirl of swearing and yelling and the clank of pots stepped a figure I was sure I recognized. Not many black men were in my acquaintance—hardly any black families lived in Lillienthal—and so for a moment I pictured the faces I knew, or had seen. With the light behind him it was hard to see his features, but after another second I was sure who it was and called out his name: "Horace!"

He squinted down the gangplank. "Who's that calling my name?" he demanded, stepping closer to the edge. He looked at me curiously—hundreds of caddies must have worked at River Hills Country Club the same years I did, and Horace worked in the clubhouse, not on the greens.

"Are you Horace?" I asked, suddenly unsure of myself, and at the same time feeling dizzy. The smell of kerosene and of the muddy river came up from the space between us, and I put my hand on a timber that stood next to the gangplank, to steady myself. Whiskey flowed through me.

"Horace Olibanum Jefford, that's right. And if you know my name, you might as well come on inside and tell us what you're doing, wandering around this old levee looking like a half-drowned river rat. Come on, step lively now!"

He reached over and pulled me across, and I stumbled a little, and then was inside the cabin he'd stepped out of, amid tied-up bedrolls and wicker trunks and pans hung on a long trestle.

"This here is Sneezewood McKenna, and Ralph Scott. And this nasty-looking creature is my son James—don't you call him Jimmy—and somewhere or t'other is Curtis Stringfellow."

The men, who were seated around a table in the middle of the cabin, looked up from their cards and mumbled howdy, all except James, who stared at me close-mouthed. They were smoking, and the smoke was like a canopy over the table. Next to it was a stove as big as a sofa, and a sink, and vegetables and fruit in baskets, all in what seemed like one pile against the wall.

"Well?" Horace raised his eyebrows.

I came to myself enough to mumble my own name, and to tell Horace I'd seen him at the club. And I told him I was going to New Orleans.

At this the other men looked up again from the table, and James showed some teeth, and one of them, I think it was Sneezewood, said: "People all the while dying to come up north. What do you want to be heading the other direction for?" There was a pause. "Of course, he continued, going back to his cards, "some folks have more trouble traveling than others."

Horace said, "Now, now," and I suddenly felt foolish, and thought what *am* I running off for, me so white and comfortable and all.

Then the boat gave a heave, as if the barge had bounced against it, and Horace said, "Current's turning. Better get at it." He looked at me quick and said, "You want some coffee," and took a cup from the trestle and a pot from the stove and put me off to the side to drink it. The boat moved again, and the men threw down their cards and together moved out the door.

"You, caddy . . . you stay here, and when we get back we'll talk about New Orleans!" He winked at James, who hadn't got up with the other men, but stayed at the table, his face rocking in the light, looking at me out of the brownest eyes I'd ever seen.

James was then eighteen, which meant he could drink and work on the river as a dealer. He was on his way south "to do a little business." When I knew him better and kidded him about the phrase, he'd laugh back at me, his laughter coming out from behind one of the cheroots he was always smoking. Cards were his business, and had been from an early age.

He got up from the table, and I could see he was taller than I was by an inch or so, rangy and wide-shouldered, with long arms—I thought of a spider.

"My papa doesn't know I'm in the life, so don't say nothing." He was rinsing out his glass at the sink as he said this, not looking at me, and his words fell from nowhere, landed nowhere, floated in the thick sweet air. He was shaking his head, and after a moment he did turn. He came back and took another look at me.

"You know what I mean?" he asked.

I didn't, exactly. I was excited in a way I hadn't been excited before, and waited to hear what else he might say.

"Forget it," he finally said, and sat down again.

Then Horace came back in and put on a yellow slicker over his jacket, and said the river was rising.

"So what about it, young bub? What's waiting for you in New Or-*leans*?" He stood at the door, expecting an answer.

"I'm going to school down there—college," I said, get-

49

ting a hold of a lie by the tail and starting to twist it. "I go to Tulane University, and I had to come home for a while, and now I'm going back."

Father and son looked at one another, and then looked back at me.

"Well, that sounds right," said Horace.

James had pulled out a nail file and was moving it across his nails, frowning down at his hands. I imagined he was about twenty-five. I couldn't take my eyes off him.

Horace said, "James here is headed down that way himself. You sure you're not running away from something? No officers of the law after your little tail?"

Sneezewood came back in the cabin and, hearing Horace, made a loud guffaw. Then he put his lips together and shook his head. "What do you think we got here, a convicted felon?" He and James laughed.

"You never do know," Horace put in mildly, and seemed satisfied no trouble would come sniffing his way. He sat down at the table and picked up the cards.

"All right, then. When that barge gets done bumping up against us and knocking off my brand-new paint, it's going down the river. And James is going to be on it, and the captain—he's a real bulldog—can take along another boy if I say so." He pulled a card out of his hand and flipped it onto the table.

"And I guess I say so." He looked at James.

"That all right with you, James?"

James spread his hands apart, shrugged his shoulders, said, "Makes me no never mind," and then giving it up, showed me a wide grin. The cabin rocked once more, Curtis Stringfellow made his appearance, blocking the doorway, as big and important as the night itself, and then James and I were down the gangplank, and across another one, and on our way.

❖

The river was wide, and the river was long. By the time we got to the Missouri border the next day I felt as if I'd been on it all my life. We kept out of the way of Captain Eugene, who I gathered regarded us as no more or less interesting than the cargo that came on with us— soybeans from Clinton, wheat and alfalfa.

We slept next to the boiler that night, and nothing we said could be heard over its clanking, the repeated stanzas of iron grating against iron. I woke up and saw James watching me—we weren't very far apart, one bunk space between us—and he offered me a drink from a little silver flask he carried in his jacket, and I remember I took it from him just so I could touch his skin. I couldn't go back to sleep then, and we both were half sitting up, the early-morning light slipping in, and as long as he was looking at me I was looking at him—as if we were both laughing, but neither of us was even smiling. The boiler chugged on, and no room for words; I sat up all the way and turned and leaned across to him, and handed back the flask—he took it, and kept hold of my hand with it, and the current ran through us both, and we bounced toward each other, and that was that.

One boy who thought he was pretty smart being outdone and outclassed, and turned, as Coach Mannucci used to say, every which way but loose. Other boy playing, then getting serious, playing again. I saw I knew nothing at all about giving someone pleasure, and I tried to do better, again and again. James was pleasure. Hot snake-smelling skin, knots of muscles hitting me like snowballs, breath like gin and jasmine—he was everything at once.

Whatever I'd been going to New Orleans for, I'd found by St. Louis. When we finally got out on deck—which wasn't a deck at all but a big flat iron field moving through the water, lines looped all across it, and nowhere to walk but along the gangways—the captain grunted good morning, and the ugly little river towns spilled out their undersides like bunting. I was ready to take on the world, whatever the world happened to be.

But by then I was thinking about my family, wondering what they were thinking. James told me he lived off and on with his mother in Chicago, and didn't see his father but once or twice a year—he'd been staying on the *River Queen* with him for a week, before starting downriver to ply his trade on the gambling boats there—and he had older brothers whom he never saw. He was so out in the world, compared to where I was, that it seemed the world was written all over him, and he fairly glowed with it.

We stood behind the lines. The wind coming up from

the south had a chance of spring in it, but the day was cold, no matter the clean white clouds snapping overhead, the bright blue tunnel of sky.

I took a breath and told him that I wasn't actually going back to school at Tulane, that I was just going to New Orleans plain and simple.

He let out a long low whistle.

"And your mama? She know that's where you're bound? Or did you just happen to run off without telling anybody?"

As pleased with me as he had seemed in the cabin, now he seemed as angry. He pulled away and walked along the gangway, and I followed after him.

When he turned around, it appeared the dark of his eyes had spilled over into the whites, they were so somber, so full of hurt.

"I thought you and me were going to be a team for a while," he said. "I thought you were your own man, but now I see you ain't even dry behind the ears."

I was confused, reached out for his arm, but he pulled it away, stood there looking at me with such reproach I felt I'd fallen overboard and was drowning.

Then he relented, said in a milder tone, "Nobody goes off and leaves their family, less they have a reason. Nobody lets them worry and carry on and wonder if they're dead or alive. Nobody I want to meet."

The softer voice eased the weight of his disapproval not at all; I was wretched. My brave freedom purchased at the price of my parents' worry hadn't been such a grand thing to achieve after all. Wouldn't they be calling the hospital by now?

I must have looked as bad as I felt, for he pulled me to him.

"Don't think I want to let you go, but seems like I'm going to have to." Then he turned me around and pushed me back toward the cabin.

"Time's got to be right," he said, and went to ask Captain Eugene how long before we tied up in East St. Louis. And that was how long we stayed in the cabin, pressed together, pulling the future out of each other, sweating and groaning and making sure each of us remembered.

When we stepped off the barge together, he walked me to the Greyhound bus station, and we sat drinking awful coffee till it was time for me to go. I got my dad when I called home, and though he too was angry, it wasn't as bad as James being angry, and I didn't have to talk to my mother at all. Dad let me know he was relieved I was all right—that was the main thing, he said.

The waitress behind the counter kept her eye on us while we sat there, and I finally realized we were in the south, or nearly. People looked at me more than they looked at James, it seemed, and I thought of what Sneezewood had said, and wondered suddenly if he would be all right. I had already made up my mind that I'd go to New Orleans after school was out—then I would be my own man—and he had given me his mother's address, and I had given him mine.

The bus north was called—I couldn't understand the announcement, but James could—and we got up and walked toward the gate.

"I'm sorry," I said to him, and couldn't think of what more.

"Well, maybe it's all right," he said, and smiled, and put his hand on my shoulder. "And I'm sorry, too, for thinking you was in the life."

Then I laughed, and said I guessed I was in it now, and he liked that, and that's how we said goodbye.

The bus rolled out and I watched him through the window, and he got smaller and smaller. We turned the corner, and he was gone.

The trip downriver stayed with me. I moved through Lillienthal in fits and starts, getting through to graduation. It was as if I'd been inflated with a gas that had me bobbing through the streets like a circus balloon. New ideas and new faces kept occurring to me, rushing down like meteors, littering the front lawn and the fields around me.

My parents had been surprisingly philosophical about my running off. My father blamed it mostly on drink. So I slipped away as one cliché and came back as another. My brothers thought it odd of me, although Franklin had, a few years back, been discovered with his sheets tied together, ready to step out through the window on Oak Street, and been slowly and reasonably talked out of his own journey. We were all prepped for departure: Dad always said he didn't want any of us living at home once we were grown, that two adult males were too many for any one house. Thinking of this, I wondered if I'd been too sentimental about coming back.

Drinking was a sporting endeavor in Lillienthal, and many stories worked their way through its boozy depths. My father had a scar on the back of his head from one night in Peoria—I remember him sitting at the kitchen table, and Mom standing behind him, swabbing it with iodine. He told us he'd been in a bar with some other men, on a business trip, and he'd been sitting in a chair with his feet up, and somebody had come by and knocked them down. Plausible, plausible. We were out-raged that anyone should have laid a hand on him; who would dare? Drinking we knew had come into it. Drink-ing had come into it when Mrs Maxwell had her hysterec-tomy, and when Mr Maxwell didn't come home, and drinking had most certainly come into it when Mrs Ryan's brother Willie had been arrested. And now, drinking had come into it with me.

Part of being an artist was drinking—and part of being a man. It wasn't good that I had run away from home, but it would've been worse if I hadn't been drinking. Drink-ing was a net that descended and caught one, a familiar bugaboo that kept other bugaboos obscured. If drinking wasn't exactly patriotic, it was a long way from being un-American. (On the television screen those early high school years, we saw Senator Joe McCarthy and a gallery full of yes-men investigating and reinvestigating the mo-tives and morals of the hapless few writers and academics and entertainers who'd been called communists by other writers and academics and entertainers. One of the charges was fleshed out by the assertion that the accused "never drank." Something suspicious about abstinence, clearly.) The boys who'd come back from the Korean War were notorious drinkers; we'd see them coming out of Mizlo's Tap, weaving down the street, hollering, their arms around one another's shoulders. Their Korean silk jackets bobbed along; the villages north and south of the famous 38th Parallel shone like small white blossoms on their backs.

My brother Franklin drank, up at school, where he had joined a fraternity. He told me how one night he and the other brothers drove off with a whole houseful of furniture they'd carried out of a model home on the edge of town, carting it back to the fraternity annex in a pickup truck. He told me about how they'd all got drunk one weekend and had an "orgy" with two girls who were in town with Shipstad & Johnson's Ice Follies. I went up to see him one weekend that spring, and got as drunk as the rest of them, but no orgies or burglaries occurred, only a Saturday night of endless dispassionate necking and Ray Coniff albums played over and over. I was with somebody's sister, who disappeared at midnight.

The fraternity house was an inappropriate setting in which to tell my brother what I'd really done when I took off for New Orleans, but I did tell him. He listened, and said I should do whatever I felt like, but I could see he was perplexed. What about Sammy? he asked.

I couldn't tell him any more than I knew myself. I told him what had happened, without going too far into the details—I realized the details weren't what he wanted to hear. His listening had the effect of making it matter-of-fact, and for that I was grateful. I had begun to be afraid of the future, afraid of it tilting and sliding back on me, or not exactly afraid, but unsure; I felt myself getting more and more attenuated, and sometimes thought I might blow away entirely. Franklin's calmness kept the freak in me at arm's length—a weird nocturnal specter like the hermaphrodite on the midway, its leering face half rouge, half stubble—and I was able to drive back down to Lillienthal with my equilibrium restored. I saw, though, that to keep my self-image from getting too garish, I had to keep the externals neat and wholesome. You could do what you liked, so long as you kept it your own affair.

I dreamed of James, and woke to take finals in history and natural science. I wound up escorting Kimberly Taylor to the senior prom; she wore tennis shoes and sweat socks with her formal gown, which we thought a great hoot. We went swimming at the club afterward, and necked as the sun was coming up. Kimberly knew my heart wasn't in it, but didn't seem to mind—it was like turning the radio on, providing the background music that maybe wasn't your favorite but would do.

Numbly we moved toward graduation, some of us bored, some of us excited by the prospect of a college career. I called information in New Orleans late one night and tried to get James's number there, but there was no listing. I tried to write letters to him, but they didn't sound like me at all—or, rather, they sounded too much like me; I couldn't write in anything but breezy. And breezy wasn't at all how I felt about him, about us. But I sent him a letter anyway, written on a Gauguin notecard I'd got from the Art Institute, saying I missed him, saying I wanted to come get a job in New Orleans that summer. . . . I drove down to the levee at night, and sat in the car: I saw lights on the *River Queen*, but never went on board. . . . I played Johnny Mathis and Elvis Presley records over and over, and discovered Laverne Baker, and played her "Jim Dandy" till even my brother Dennie Lee complained. And lifted weights and did a hundred sit-ups, and wondered how I'd look with long hair. The summer got nearer and nearer.

Finally, I heard from James. His letter came the day after I received word that I'd been accepted at Iowa City. I had, in the twenty-four hours between letters, nearly convinced myself that an Iowa college was what I wanted. It was what my parents wanted for me: a career that would successfully blend creativity and practicality. I had no trouble seeing myself as an Advertising Man.

But then my enthusiasm abruptly jumped the track, fell silent beside it as the engine of my deeper desire came hurtling through. James wrote that he was staying in a rooming house in the Quarter, and that I could come and stay there too. He said he had been lucky with the cards, that he was working on the river, weekends. He said he would be happy to see me! It was all I needed to rearrange my plans, my life.

My parents didn't want to hear about New Orleans. Their plans for me had to do with an interview Dad had arranged for me across the river. If all went well, I was to work as an apprentice in a small agency, learning pasteup and copy, getting the jump on my college classmates.

It wasn't the summer I saw before me. I saw James and only James. I was coming on fast toward my eighteenth birthday, and was as full of myself as a tree is full of sap.

College and commercial art weren't at all what I had in mind, not for that summer, maybe not for that fall either. If I could just get away and put myself in the way of a more romantic sort of experience, I could become the person I wanted to be. Nothing could have stopped me from getting out of Iowa. And nothing did.

New Orleans in early summer, with the sun shining through the balconies of the French Quarter, creating blocks of swirling Arabic letters on the brick and stucco walls behind them, mixing chirping patois and languid Gullah with the broad flat vowels of Texarkana, confounding the eye and ear at every corner—New Orleans in June is a sweet chunk of marzipan one could chew all one's days. In late summer, that same sweetness will cloy, and produce what is known locally as the vapors, an aversion to all things warm and honeyed—women will put a dash of vinegar in their soups and bathwater; men will sprinkle cucumber and lemon into their handkerchiefs and decorously mop their brows—but that is later, later. June is a dream, crisp and clear and golden.

On Borchardt Street, where James's rooming house stood, the trees on either side branched up and met in a thicket of green and scarlet, and the light that came through the street and sidewalk below was dappled—at midday it was like walking through confetti. The flowering bushes that spread out along the fences and sent purple and yellow vines up along the clapboard wall contributed all the more to the festive aspect. Small birds darted in and out among the blossoms, and white butterflies hovered over the small vegetable patches that crept around from side gardens and thrust themselves up next to the gate.

James had gained some weight that spring. His spidery frame now seemed more that of man than boy. And his hair, which had been coarse and unruly when we met, had come under lye and pomade and lay back from his forehead in soft shining waves. When he met me at the station, he was wearing a hat, and rings on his fingers I didn't remember. But his smile was the same, and led me to him like a beacon.

We took a streetcar from the station and walked the last bit to Borchardt Street. I had brought a suitcase, stuffed with summer clothes and drawing pads, and we took turns carrying it. I was going to be an artist that summer, justify my impulse, and everywhere I turned in those shining streets and alleys I saw sketches and paintings, quick bright flashes of color.

"So now you're on your own," he said as we walked along, and he looked at me sideways, appraisingly. "And nobody's going to be worrying about you but me. . . ." It wasn't a question, and I didn't need to answer. The way he talked and the way he looked at me made me feel I'd been stitched onto him, like the sleeve on his jacket, or the band around his tan fedora. We walked slowly, and stopped once to buy shaved ice and syrup and seemed to be taking our time, but I was already in bed with him and his New Orleans life, pressed against his broad black chest, inhabiting my future.

The boardinghouse was painted a dull mustard color,

and the windows were framed in a deep green. Inside, it was dark and cool, and smelled of candles and frangipani. Someone rose from a chair.

"This is Miz Odum—Miz Odum, this is my friend Mr McGinnis."

Mrs Odum was a big woman, but delicate. She offered me a tiny warm object—her hand—which I shook, and she moved to the side of the room on two other tiny objects—her feet. Elsewhere, she was vast. There was something pleasing about the odd conjunctions of her frame, and also about the disharmony of her costume; it seemed that she had left some of herself behind, or sent it on ahead. Her hair was tied by a purple scarf, and her smock was orange and blue, and beneath it trailed a hem of vivid pink. She was here but not here, tentative as an unfinished sketch, present only as an idea of herself.

"Pleased to meet you, Mr McGinnis. Make yourself to home. You're just off the second landing there"—she waved her birdlike hand upward—"and Mr Jefford here will show you"—she bent to pick up a bit of lint, straightened with a sigh—"what's what."

She smiled, fluttered through to the hallway.

We mounted the stairs, turned past doors that opened and closed, dark male faces smiling out, around toothbrushes, within circles of shaving cream—towels adjusted, coughs interrupted, somewhere a gentle insistent swearing.

A sign on the landing read: "No Ladies Above the First Floor." James pointed to it as we passed, shook his finger in mock warning.

"Miz Odum doesn't much take to womenfolk. But she surely does love the men." He chuckled and raised his eyebrows.

We stopped, and he pushed open the door of one room, put my suitcase inside it, then closed it and opened another directly across the hall.

"That's yours, and this is mine," he said, pulling me after him across the threshold. "And this"—he indicated the great big four-poster bed in the middle of the room—"is ours!"

And didn't we ramble. The months between us fell away, and we were back on the barge again, the boiler pounding away. The church bells in the Quarter rang every hour; they took us into the night, past vespers, like the bell before each round in a prizefight, punctuating the long sweet hours of give and take, the tolling reminding us that we were somewhere in the world.

He liked saying my name, and I liked saying nothing at all, not having to say anything—just holding on. There was a sink in his room, and from time to time we splashed each other with the cool water from the tap. His lips were so sweet, and his long educated fingers so tender. From outside, along with the ringing of the bells, came other music. Musicians who played in the bars and the clubs of the Quarter stayed in the rooming houses of Borchardt Street, and Petaluma Street beyond it; we heard an olio of music up in James's room, thick and overheated, simmering through the afternoon and evening. Mrs Odum's was not a musical boardinghouse, but others nearby were. We had clarinets for robins and saxophones for bobolinks, and a big bass fiddle somewhere sounded like a bullfrog on a pond. And the children running and yelling and making mischief, and men pestering, and women eluding—all contributed to the vines of sound that rose, and trembled, and flowered in our window.

The first few days had no demarcation, eased into one another. The differences between Monday and Tuesday were negligible, after all—whoever thought up days and weeks seemed far, far away from the Quarter. I had to get a job, that was the condition of my being in New Orleans—I was meant to be making enough money, somehow, to make the whole endeavor worthwhile. But the first week had no obligations.

We spent our days and nights getting reacquainted (acquainted, really—what we knew of each other from the river was the fundamental part) and prowling through the streets and alleys, looking in on James's friends here and there, stuffing ourselves with hush puppies and gumbo and warm greasy crullers from the Café Dumond. James decided I had to have a hat, and bought me one, a white panama that was years older than I was, and I resolved to grow a mustache to go with it.

Nobody seemed to notice or care that we spent all our time together, that my bed stayed flat and unrumpled while his was a sea of wrinkled linen. Or that we kept hanging on each other and poking and cuffing and finding any excuse to keep flesh on flesh. Once we stopped at a bar, and never went back—he said people had been real friendly when he'd been there by himself, but the two of us together bottled up that good feeling: we got cold looks from the crowd and the fish-eye from a bartender. It was all men in the bar, all of them older, and shrill voices and elaborate gestures, and a kind of hissing noise when we left.

Nobody minded if we drank in the boardinghouse; we kept beer in the refrigerator and whiskey in our room, and at night when we sat down to table with the other boarders we would have a glass of wine. Mrs Odum never asked how old I was—I believe she thought that if I was old enough to be away from home and out in the world, I could do what I liked. She cooked up some spicy stews, and a lot of beer and wine went down with them.

There would be six or seven men at table, one other white face complementing mine, belonging to a Mr Chough, who had bad teeth and seldom smiled. I caught him once or twice watching me while his jaws moved up and down on the shrimp and peppers, something quizzical in his gaze, but we had no conversation. More talkative faces hovered over the blue-and-white crockery, the checkered cloth. Mr Mulkin and Mr McBride, who lived on the first floor, kept up a lighthearted exchange on the events of the day; both worked as bus conductors and had plenty to say about the comings and goings of the human race. Mr Mulkin was heavy and wore his hair cropped close to his skull; he had a thick warm laugh that we sometimes heard bubbling up from his room below us, joined by the higher, more ethereal notes of Mr McBride. Mr Harrison lived on the same floor as these two, but was irregular at table. He was younger than they, but older than we, lean as a rail, with dark hooded eyes and nervous hands. We'd see the light on when we climbed the stairs at night, with always a sweetish smell coming from under the door.

In addition to these guests there might be a suitor of

Mrs Odum's at table. Insubstantial as her spirit seemed, her fleshly appetites were down-to-earth, and considerably varied; the number of cousins and old friends that passed through was high. She had a blood nephew named Thomas who helped out in the kitchen, and on weekends Thomas's mother might come to call, but no other Odums appeared. Humming and fluttering by, our landlady moved like a burgee in the breeze. She kept house, cooked, and cleaned and managed still to look as if she lacked the authority even to boil water. She took some pride in her cuisine.

"Hand Mr McGinnis over those beets," she directed Thomas. "We want him to appreciate our New Orleans cooking."

"Do I taste coriander in this stew?" Mr Mulkin wanted to know.

"Yes indeed you do—you do know your spices, Mr Mulkin." Her broad face was fresh as a young girl's.

I found I didn't have to initiate much in the way of conversation, only let myself put in a few words now and again, smile, and eat my fill. I'd paid out enough for my first two weeks' lodging, and had enough for the rest of the month, but after that I was going to have to earn what I needed. I wasn't worried. I'd already started doing sketches, down at the end of the street in a tiny park where older women sat and sewed, or just sat, where tinkers and fishmongers stopped for a cigar and a taste of something cool. A chipped statue, whose inscription and dates were nearly rubbed off, stood in the middle of pigeons: a French hero who James told me had routed the pirates when they threatened to burn the city. The park was where we'd stopped for shaved ice my first day in town, and I soon thought of it as some place personal and special. It was best at dusk, and if James was taking a nap, I'd slip out of the house with my pad and go down.

I watched the women at their stitching, and the youngsters jumping rope. At first they all watched me, but after a few days I think I blended in. After I started work at the ribbon factory, I got to the park only after it was turning dark, or on the weekend. Sometimes it was just the old white hero and me in the gathering darkness, between the children and the women who had left and the more sporting collection of people who would come later to take their ease, after supper and beyond. I noticed how the aroma of the flowers, and all the other smells of life—the horses on the street, and even the wash still hanging from the balconies on either side, and the geraniums and cobblestones—all became stronger at dusk. That dark grainy mist that fell on the park seemed to make all sensations more vivid, and you could hear farther, breathe deeper, at twilight.

James was used to sleeping for an hour in the afternoon; he said it gave him an edge on the night, when sometimes he'd play right through till dawn, stepping off the dock on Decatur Street as the rest of the city was waking up. He worked on the *Belle* and the *Avalon* mainly, where he knew the crew and where card games were arranged as a matter of course. I tagged along the first weekend I was with him, partly because I was curious about the life, mostly because I didn't want to lose sight of him. He stood by our big bed pulling on his rings and putting himself into his sharkskin trousers, humming whatever snippet of melody had chanced to drift in at the window. Watching him dress was almost as exciting as watching him undress. When he was set to go, I walked with him down the stairs, carrying his little valise. It smelled of Florida water and talcum and had always a little half pint of whiskey in it, in case somebody needed a drink.

We four boys had played poker at home when we were growing up, and Dad had tried to teach us pinochle, but I was never much for cards, and the stakes we played for in Lillienthal were like no stakes at all, toothpicks and pennies.

The brand of cards James played was a universe away. I stood off to the side of the *Avalon* saloon and watched him, marveling at the sleek ease of his movements, the concentration on his face as he calculated and bluffed, then reached for the pot. To have him but a few yards away and not to have any contact with him—no quick glances, no wide smile flashing across the table—was disconcerting.

"Twelve on Ruby," said the dealer, and the men at the table grunted or nodded or were still.

And then, "Opal takes it over the top"—and a sigh. The players were known by their gems, a local peculiarity, and no one sat down to the gambling table unembellished.

"Eighteen on Tourmaline," the dealer went on, then, "Twenty-one!" and a belligerent chorus, a scraping of chair legs, and the refreshening of drinks.

"Tourmaline shining tonight," remarked a fat catfish of a toff, helping himself to the bourbon from the tray beside me, throwing it back, returning to the fray. Tourmaline was James.

I watched them play, and felt a swell of pride when he

won, disappointment when he lost or folded early. They played and drank, and I simply drank, and no one noticed me at all. I went out on deck and looked at the stars, and it was quiet on the water, the blackness all around thick and soupy. I could see across the river to Algiers, where a few lights still shone, and I sat down in a deck chair and watched the lights for a while, and fell asleep.

When I woke up James was standing over me, smiling.

"Looks like you don't find it all too exciting," he said, poking at my shoulder till I grabbed his hand. I felt guilty for having walked out and fallen asleep.

"Oh, no," I said, protesting. "It *is* exciting."

But he was right, and we both knew it, and it got resolved I wouldn't tag along any more nights on the *Avalon*. I imagine I didn't much like being outside the frame, with him and the others so suave and dark and beautiful in the middle of the canvas. I caught a cold from sleeping out on deck, and was sneezing and wiping my eyes for the next few days, and he was bringing me honey and lemon from the kitchen, and one way and another the balance got restored.

James was the youngest of seven children, and all his brothers and sisters were ranged across the country. Two of the sisters were living in Chicago with his mother; the brothers were in Kansas City and Atlanta, and his father had for forty years or so been working at River Hills Country Club, living here and there around Lillienthal, and on the river. His mother worked two jobs in Cottage Grove, on the south side of Chicago, and he had lived with her till he finished high school, then stepped out on his own. He was a year older than I, but had collected authority in ways that made him seem more than that—he had a cousin who was in and out of reform school who had taught him all about his own equipment. James told me about how he and Rudolph would hang out together, and how Rudolph had an older white friend who used to take photographs of the two boys, playing with each other and whatnot.

"Used to go down on us too," he said, stroking my back as we lay together in his big pink bed, drinking bourbon, spreading out our past.

It was the first time I'd heard the phrase, and it could've meant so many things, I was a little disappointed when he told me what it did mean. Putting a phrase on a thing didn't enhance it much, I noticed. There weren't two others like us in the world, we were unique and fabulous. All the rest was static and nonsense. I found I didn't want to hear about him and Rudolph, not how they shot craps together or engaged in this and that bit of petty larceny in the Loop, nor how they worked up the photographer, or salesman, or deli man together.

"Didn't he cry uncle?" he mused, remembering the reaction of so and so, who had wanted him to settle down in Oak Park. Something about the rope of his conquests, the string of his previous partners, wound too tight.

Besides, I hadn't much to tell him about my own experiences. My life as a homophile was only beginning. I felt proud of myself when I was with him in a way I hadn't before—easier to be proud of what you are when you have someone to be proud of it with. Walking down Bourbon Street, sitting at the dock on Decatur, or calling on his friends on Esplanade—anywhere we went, something seemed to follow us, some kind blue light that made us shine. The music of the streets was high and tender, and it rang us up and down the streetcar lines. Women reached for us out of their open doorways as we passed: whatever it was we were demonstrating, people wanted to buy.

Mrs Odum would remark, "You boys look mighty spiffy tonight," adding to the remark one of her quick sighs. I loved wearing a hat when we went out in the evening. James had picked up eye-catching items of apparel that he wore with style: a velvet vest with little pearl buttons that was as smart as anything on the river, a pair of deep-red suede shoes with Cuban heels. He moved through New Orleans with a graceful lope. It seemed he was always scooping up the air as he passed—he had played basketball, he had known how to run through the streets—and his smile was like his armor. His spirit and his body were one, and that to me was magical, remembering his long lean authority, remembering the night air, the river and the honeysuckle, the smell of his skin that was like all of it together. When I was drawing in the park, or just sitting on the dock and watching the boats go by, I was thinking of him, and the sense of rightness and fullness that came from what we had together carried me along.

Then the third week—it might have been the third year, so intense was every moment—I got a job.

Little Mr McBride knew someone who worked at Regalia Manufacturing, a ribbon factory in his old neighborhood, and he had heard they might be hiring. He presented this fact at dinner.

"Taking anybody," he said, "even northern boys, I expect."

He liked to have his joke about northern and southern, by which I guess he meant white and black. I got the feeling that the men at Mrs Odum's were all somewhat enamored of James—Mr McBride included—but they never said anything outright that let me know they were jealous. McBride was good-natured, and handsome in his small impish way. He had learned from Mrs Odum to make sweet potato pie, and for two nights we'd had it for dessert.

"Printing ribbons for prizewinners and for the county fair. You go talk to Darnell Weeks." He said he'd take me out on his busline the next day.

I had another slice of pie, and considered, and looked to James for his opinion.

"Young ar-teests do have to eat," he said.

So I rode out with Mr McBride on his lurching blue-and-tan bus, and got off twenty minutes from Borchardt Street. I spoke with Mr Darnell Weeks and he said they'd try me out, and then I was taking that bus every morning, inside a working life.

The factory was on three floors, and the top floor was where I worked: white and black boys together, women sitting at their spooling tables, winding and winding.

Below us, trophies were boxed and the gray cardboard boxes of PRIDE OF PLACE and CHAMPION and RUNNER-UP got labeled and dispatched.

The spools of color hung from the wall—blue firsts, red seconds, yellow thirds, white, then pink, finally green. We got our work orders from Louie at the type table, whose hands moved over the drawers absently, who grinned and chewed gum, his eyes always on the ladies. Louie was Cajun. He sang in a high-pitched whine over the sound of the machines and the chatter. His thing was taking out his dick with one hand while he was setting type with the other, keeping a conversation up with the woman roller he had his side to. The high desk was a screen between them. From where we six or seven men stood against the wall, on his other side, we could see him pulling on it, spitting in his hand, shooting us a sly wink. I had to be cool and not too fascinated when he first did it. Roscoe to my left said it happened once or twice a week, I should pay him no mind.

Roscoe was my age and already married with two children. His wife worked down on the second floor, and the kids stayed home with her parents. She's only going to work another month or so, he told me, or, another week or so, or, sometimes, just till the end of summer. He was disgusted with Louie, and expected me to be, too. When Louie took it out, Roscoe would set his jaw and glower at him, as if all the women on all the floors were being demeaned by him, not just the roller of the moment. The other men on the line were unperturbed.

The work wasn't difficult, but we were on our feet all day, and the bending and pulling tired me out. The air was thick with the smell of sizing, and bits of gold leaf clung to every surface; it was under my fingernails and in my hair when I came home every afternoon.

An old white man named Harris was the foreman and walked among the workers frowning and complaining and blowing his nose in his gray handkerchief when he was especially upset. The years of surveillance had dropped his chin low on his chest, and his back rose behind his neck in an odd hump. He was a short man, with no authority in his bearing, and the workers generally ignored him.

I came home flattened out, but James would cheer me up. I tried to do some drawing in the evening, but it seemed there was always something else going on. It was a job, and I was glad I had it, but it taxed my body more than I imagined it could. It was like the first days of football practice back in Lillienthal, when you practiced early in the morning and then in the early evening, and in between lay around the house trying to consolidate your strength.

We went to Tipitina's club the weekend after I started at Regalia, and I was still feeling sluggish and heavy-limbed. My shoulders and back hadn't yet got used to the pulling pressure of the press handles. A knot had developed on my right shoulder near the neck, and at one point in the evening James leaned across the table, smiling through the welter of Dixie beer bottles and fried peanuts, and massaged it. And that made me feel proud and happy, that he didn't care who saw. The club was smoky, and the man on the piano had a round mouth and the songs came out like bubbles from a fish. Everything was underwater. James moved like a shark, coming up close and then fading back; the waitresses danced like waves. We were crowded into the tiny room with a hot Saturday-night crowd, and the music was pumping up and down:

> . . . *and when you come to New Orleans*
> *You will see the Zulu King . . .*

coming through the sweet sticky air. They called the piano player Professor, and he kept on squeezing the notes: they flew out of the piano like squirts of lemon, hit the walls and the ceiling and the happy faces. He rode the piano, and the young, broad-shouldered men behind him slapped at their drums and guitar, all of them nearing the finish together.

The music was the closest to the earth that I'd been— the swaying, bouncing crowd kept my face right against it. The sort of music you could smell and taste, the kind that swirled you around in its vortex, pulled something out of you that you didn't know was there. James stood behind me when the tables got too crowded, tight in the middle of a netful of shining arms and faces, white sleeves rolled up over muscles of midnight blue, men with their women standing pressed against them, women in scarlet and mustard-colored dresses, in terry-cloth halters and pedal pushers, a crowd coming out of its shoes. The Professor would throw his notes toward one or another of the couples, and they would shout them back, and the rinky-tink sound of it all was something thrilling.

Hard and fast, like a storm at sea, and the music rose up in higher and higher waves, with James rocking and sweating behind me, and then things all tilted sideways, and were quiet.

I came to in what must have been the manager's office, the photos of various jazz greats slowly coming into focus over the couch where I lay. James was bending over me, concern all over his face, and his brown eyes as big as I had ever seen them.

"Giving me a turn here, Mickey," he said, and I saw there were some other men standing behind him, waiters probably, and as I started to sit up, one of them came forward and motioned me to stay where I was.

"Too much heat," he said in a low rumbling voice, and gave James a wink. "You all right now—but you better have your friend here carry you home and put you to bed."

He was grinning so hard that I had to sit up to prove I wasn't some little pasty-face. James wasn't crazy about his smirk either, I could tell.

"That's all right," James said, exaggeratedly polite in the midst of innuendo. He asked was I fit enough to get up and come home, and naturally I said I was.

The man still stood over me, and he was taller and

heavier than James, with a smile that you might call nasty, but you would not call unattractive.

Get me out of here, I thought.

❖

The next morning, I felt embarrassed, as if I'd behaved badly, gotten drunk. Maybe I had gotten drunk. People did, after all, pass out. But the guilt I felt wasn't so much to do with what I'd done as what I hadn't. It had to do with the big slick-looking bouncer at the club, with wanting him to crawl right on top of me while I lay on that couch. This was something new, something I hadn't had to deal with before now. Up until that moment, I hadn't seen anybody but James. Up until then, I'd thought I was set for life.

I got back to drawing in the park again, the next few days when James went overnight on the *Avalon*, up to Vicksburg and back. I was drawing the white statue, giving it more life than it had, filling up the paper around it with oleanders and dark faces, getting it wrong and starting up again. One of the sketches I produced looked like a real drawing when I finished it, and I put it up in James's room, stuck under the rim of the mirror. When he came back, he professed to like it a great deal, and that made me keep on.

I got the idea I'd like to draw him sitting in the park, and I couldn't tell if he thought that was an especially good idea or not, but he agreed. Next afternoon, when I came home from Regalia, and after his nap, I sat facing him on the wooden bench, and tried to get his fine dark features down. Trying so hard, I made a mess of him again and again; a lot of other faces began to peep through the smudges of pencil and Conté, but none of them was his. I wouldn't let him see my little stack of failures, threw them into the backyard trash can before dinner. But the next afternoon I tried again, and finally something came through that *might* have been his brother or his cousin. But he didn't even see that resemblance when I relented and showed it to him.

"Why don't you just use your imagination?" he suggested after wrinkling and unwrinkling his nose, giving the sheet of paper a long look of disapproval. "I know your imagination's a powerful thing."

But that's not what I wanted to do. I wanted to draw him from life, not memory, and I got short-tempered and said I'd do it my way, and drew something ugly and beady-eyed the next time, and finally decided that was enough of that.

James was proud of his looks, and my not doing them justice must have been like denying the veracity of that handsome charm. You look into a mirror that gives you back a distorted image, quick enough you look away. I felt something lacking in me, in not being able to catch his likeness—not so much a lack of talent as a lack of affection. I had to get him down.

Work at the factory plodded along, the July heat becoming steamy and uncomfortable. Roscoe disappeared for two days in the middle of the week, mumbled about trouble at home when he came in again. Darnell Weeks fired a girl in the trophy department because she was taking home as many pieces as she engraved, little bitty things she stuck in her purse, like statuettes from a midway; she just had to have her own collection.

The presses wheezed and sighed and clanked, and at night it took me a good number of drinks before I felt my ordinariness slip away, my sense of uniqueness return. The more time I put in, away from James and away from my drawing, the less I felt I inhabited an adventure that was mine (ours) alone. The pattern I was setting for myself at Regalia seemed decidedly humdrum.

James was a glamorous figure, but was I? Could glamour rub off? If it could I was. Otherwise, I had to admit, as the 4-H streamers passed beneath my fingers and the other Regalia workers spat and swore, glamour was elsewhere. I might as well have stayed in Lillienthal and gone to work across the river at Hamilton Beach. It was only when I brought James into the picture I saw of my life that it brightened, took on colors other than the dirty blues and purples of the ribbon factory. Through him, I was learning things about myself, about the life of the senses, and at a rapid clip. This I knew was what an artist was obliged to do.

And I was earning my own way in the world, a not inconsiderable satisfaction. Most of all I felt the pleasure of spending my emotions, emotions hoarded so long— and I delighted in the fine soaring freedom, the solidifying of my amatory intent.

❖

Lillienthal was hundreds of miles upriver, with tiny figures going about tiny chores. Here in New Orleans I was
larger than my previous life. My younger brothers Dennie
Lee and Chris sent me letters; they were now working as
caddies the way Franklin and I had. I realized how
quickly they were coming up behind us—and I suppose
that, too, boosted my feeling of freedom. As if, by filling
our shoes, they'd let us step out of them, move on. Franklin was living at home, between college semesters, working at the Alcoa plant. I wondered how he felt about his
own freedom. What was the same about us and what was
different had got hard to determine.

Dennie Lee wrote most often, and James asked me to
read these letters to him. James was enthralled with the
idea of younger brothers. Being the youngest himself,
he'd never had the chance to baby any of his siblings—
he had never expected from, but always been expected
of. And he wanted to counsel, to expect; he often talked
to me about doing this or that with my life, using my
imagination, fulfilling my potential. No doubt his expectations were too high. Sometimes he sounded like Mr
Adams, the vice-principal back in high school. All I
had in mind to do was soak up life, become in turn all
the vivid colors that came my way, never mind about
potential.

What resolve I had had hardened into a determination
to see all I could, to do all I might, and to worry about
putting it to use, sorting it out, later. If I was lucky, then I
deserved to be lucky; wasn't that the way it went?

❖

It got to be Sunday afternoon, then, in late July, with James upstairs asleep, and me down on my park bench, thinking about my brothers, making a series of desultory passes with my pencil, wishing I could be more inspired. Usually I would have been in the boardinghouse at this hour, or out with James calling on friends and players. But he was exhausted from running up and down the river, and he hadn't done too well at the tables either, so he was sleeping off Mrs Odum's pork roast and his discontent, and I was marking time.

Women who usually sat in the park on weekdays were home now with their families; children who played kick-the-can next to the entrance gate were drowsing on their daddies' knees. Everything was still, except for the blue jays who kept on with their usual disclaimers, contending with the church bells and the notes of a listless piano that came from the direction of Beaufort Street.

"Well, now, you look recovered."

Some familiar voice coming low and wet from behind me; a man standing in a patch of speckled sunlight beside the bench. Big and powerful-looking. Smiling in a way that said he knew something I didn't, but I'd find out soon enough.

"Mind if I sit down?"

It was the bouncer from Tipitina's.

"Make yourself comfortable," I said. Suddenly I was alert, roused from my torpor. I felt the presence of sex and danger at once, cool air flowing over me, tingling my flesh.

"You all by yourself this afternoon, huh? Seems like I'm in the same situation. My lady doing her social duties today, letting me fend for myself, so to speak."

He was leaning back against the bench now, blue serge slacks pulling tight over his thighs, a polka-dot shirt gapping here and there down the front. His hair was slick with pomade, and he had a gold-capped tooth that shone in his smile; around his neck was a chain hung with small charms, amulets. The smell of peaches, of sharp cologne, talc.

He looked down at my drawing pad, then around the park.

"What sort of drawing you do? Not much here to look at, that's the truth. Draw some of this nightlife here in the Quarter, get some of this here local color." He laughed, a low rumbling sound that got inside you, made your skin dance. I felt his magnetism, his sexual energy. He leaned a little closer, lowered his voice, let it boil slowly, confidentially. I was feeling fidgety, uncomfortable, stuck to the moment like a fly on flypaper.

"Too hot out here by half. What do you say we take a walk over to my crib? It's not far, just over toward Jackson. Get us a little re-lax-a-tion." He winked as he articulated each syllable, and my face got hot, and he laughed to see the color there. Maybe, if I didn't say anything in compliance, it wouldn't be my fault. Maybe I could just drift along. . . .

His crib, as he called it, was a basement apartment, small and dark, with a dressmaker's dummy in the corner and sheets of paper stuck with pins on a big red upholstered chair. He switched on an electric fan that had little strips of ribbon hanging from it, got out a bottle of gin, and poured two glasses.

"Here's to it," he said, and drained the glass in one motion, then reached over and pulled me against him.

"Feel that?" he wanted to know, his lips moving against my ear. "That's what all these women wanting hereabouts. . . . Gonna give you some today, see what you can do with it."

He pulled back, and I took as much gin as I could swallow. He looked at me till I looked away, and his trousers came off like the skin off a banana, and I got scared for a moment, but that passed, and then he took charge and I just let it happen, getting hotter and hotter the guiltier I felt. His joint was like a forearm and a fist, the kind you see drawn on rest-room walls, in eight-page bibles, never expect to see in life. Not up close.

"Bigger it is, the easier it is," he was saying, stretching me out on the carpet. Some little fluffy yellow cat had come out of the shadows, and stood watching; I stared at its face as mine bent backward. With James, sex was give and take and a lot of caring. This wasn't anything to do with that, this was winding me and unwinding me like a top, seeing how much and for how long; playing with a rag doll that didn't protest.

More gin, and more: deadening the image of my sweet James. Here I was, learning about life, taking a good long drink at the well of the senses. And hearing the bells of St. George's, closer than on Borchardt Street, so close they seemed to come from inside my own head. Feeling they might crack the walls of my skull wide open, keep me crazy and freakish, for good and always.

It was late when I finally pulled away from Leopold and out of his sticky lair, so late the stars were out and the moon was filling up with light and the night birds were busy in the trees. It might be James was still asleep and I could keep mum; maybe you did something like this and just walked away from it. Dad had once said that a man has to take his actions upon himself, and keep them to himself—that telling all and whining for forgiveness only put the burden on somebody else. Was that true?

Back at Mrs Odum's the supper plates were still clean on the table in the dining room, and the sound of Thomas watching TV in the kitchen seemed to me reassuring, calming. I crept up the stairs, but caught the glances of Mr Mulkin and Mr McBride, who were sitting in the parlor playing checkers. I felt they could see everywhere my body had been and everything it had done in the last few hours. But they were gentlemen, and seeing me creeping in so furtively, pretended they didn't see me at all.

Upstairs, the light was off in James's room, and that was when I should have left well enough alone. But I was in a state, and had to be sure everything was as it was before my adventure—that was a good word for it—and so I pushed his door open and peeked inside.

"Mickey? I been wondering where you all got off to. Come over here. Come on. . . ." He was propped up in bed, with no light but the moonlight coming through the window, and I couldn't tell how long he'd been awake.

In that light, there was something catlike about his eyes, the deep brown shining with a milky blue. I came to him and lay down beside him.

"I'm sorry I've been outside so long. Just drawing, out in the park, trying to get something done. . . ."

He didn't say anything in reply, and I pressed close against him. He'd thrown off the sheet and lay smooth and naked in the patch of moonlight, and I thought, This is a painting, this is art, just this.

In a soft voice he asked, "Where's your drawing pad?" His hands weren't moving on my body the way they usually did; he was waiting, hanging in the moonlight.

I'd left my pad at Leopold's. Thrown in the chair with his old lady's dress patterns. Left behind, forgotten.

"Gotta get a new one," I said, in my squeaky little voice. "Used it all up."

"I bet you did," he said, slow and deliberate. He sat up, facing away from me on the other side of the bed. "Better take a shower," he said in a flat voice I'd never heard before, "'cause you be smelling like something out of a whorehouse."

He was up and pulling on his slacks and shirt, bending over to lace up his suede shoes.

"James . . ." I didn't know what words would come out of my mouth, but the panic I felt was something I had to cover over.

"I don't want to hear it. Whatever you think you gotta say, you go tell it to the wall."

He was standing by the door now, and I jumped out of bed and tried to put my arms around him, but he pulled away. And I guess he saw in my face the fear and panic and shame, and maybe he relented a little; for a minute, he let me hold on to him.

Then he was out the door and down the stairs. And I wasn't half of something glorious anymore; I wasn't sure and proud and invincible—I was shivering and cold in an overheated room in New Orleans, somebody small and insignificant and alone, somebody who's just thrown away more than he knew he had.

Next morning, I got up out of that pink bed and went to work as usual. Crying through the night hadn't done me any good, and waiting for James to come back made the minutes hours, and I couldn't take it. I would go off to Regalia, and when I came home in the afternoon, he'd be there again, and he'd understand I was miserable about going off; he'd forgive me, and everything would be fine.

It was a humid morning; the men at the factory had their shirts off by ten o'clock. The Louisiana State Fair had sent in a rush order for cattle and poultry rosettes and badges, and old Harris was rushing back and forth, exhorting the women to clean it up, clean it up.

Just before noon, when there was a temporary lull, I saw out of the corner of my eye that Louie had leaned back in his chair and was giving his nether self an airing. He looked over at us, to make sure he had a gallery, but only Roscoe and I seemed to be aware of him, busy as all the rest were, lining up their Firsts and Seconds and Honorable Mentions. And I saw that Roscoe was in a state himself, as if the steam coming off the type were rolling off his head and shoulders, as if he were some kind of animal about to jump.

The clack-clack of the presses covered the words he was saying—I could only see his mouth working and the muscles of his jaw clenching and unclenching. He turned to look, and abruptly turned back to his press, letting the length of red ribbon he was printing fall beside him. He leaned forward for a moment and pressed his forehead against the wall, and I could see a tremor moving across his shoulders.

Then he wheeled around and came at Louie with his line of type, brandishing it above his head like a hammer. He was yelling and swearing, and Louie stood up so fast to ward him off his pants stayed in the chair. He twisted away, his joint slapping one thigh, then the other, and thrust him off. Roscoe was scrambling over the type table, Pica and English flying all around him, and I was suddenly in the middle of it, trying to pull him back. Beets, the man on the other side, was pulling with me, and it was as if Roscoe were made out of iron himself, he was so powerful. Red-eyed and furious, he fought back—the letters in his type stick were like hot glowing teeth. All the women were screaming, and the girl just on the other side of Louie's desk was looking across at him with an expression of horror and disbelief.

Harris scurried over from the far end of the long workroom. I had my eye on him as much as on Roscoe, thinking now it would all come to an end. Then Roscoe turned and caught me across the stomach with his smoldering stick.

So hot it didn't burn at first, the type left three letters on me. When I looked down I saw the S E C burned into me, and was outraged, and slumped against the table. My strength drained away. The pain came fast enough, and then I was flailing at Roscoe, with Harris and Weeks standing over us, and the other printers finally getting Roscoe's arms behind him.

The pain and the heat made me nauseous, and Beets helped me out of the pressroom into the lounge, where there was a ratty old couch I could lie down on. I could hear the loud voices, Roscoe's yelling, almost weeping, then a woman's voice—which I guessed was his wife's—rising and falling, and gradually the noise of the machines taking over again.

Weeks came in, tight-mouthed and stiff, and said they couldn't countenance brawling, and that I had better pick up my check and call it quits. Just then the door to the nearest toilet stall swung open and Louie came out, shaking his head and grinning, but looking worried when he saw the blisters on my stomach. He told Weeks it wasn't my fault, that Roscoe had come after him, and that he was surely indebted to me for helping him out. Weeks looked dubious but grudgingly accepted his words, and I came to understand I wasn't fired after all.

Louie got some salve from the office and patted it on the burn, and wrapped gauze around me, humming his bayou melodies all the while. His tobacco-stained fingers were softer, gentler than I would have imagined, and his scratchy song was like a lullaby. It was all his fault of course, but I felt my anger coming undone as he patted my skin. He leaned close enough that I could smell the tobacco on his breath, his solicitude easing my stinging pain that ought to have been his.

They told me to take the rest of the day off. Louie walked downstairs with me and said again how sorry he was, and we shook hands. I said it wasn't his fault, really. I wondered whose fault it was. Roscoe was clearly out of himself, and you couldn't blame craziness, could you? Blame evaporated in the air, along with the smell of sizing and gold leaf. And in the pain I felt something almost ennobling: I felt the sweet sanctity of the victim.

I wasn't fired, but I knew I wasn't going back to Regalia. I sat out on the back porch, listening to Thomas in the kitchen as he chuckled and snickered at the dancers on "American Bandstand." A blond girl named Franny was striking attitudes on the Philadelphia dance floor, part jitterbug, part twist, being cute and oblivious: living for the camera. The sound of Sam Cooke's high clear tenor came out to me as I sat waiting for James. *Bring it, bring it on home to me* ringing out lustrous and lyrical, floating over the hydrangeas and the sweet peas. And I leaned against the rickety balcony and knew it was over, all of it: the summer, my life in New Orleans, the spiraling freedom that had tossed me around one time too often.

Through the screen door I watched as Franny's smooth pout gave way to the smiling face of Dick Clark, and I looked away, and wondered, in the fullness of my disillusion and self-pity, what was to become of me after all.

I left New Orleans after James. I left it smoking in the midmorning heat, left it the way I'd come, and headed upriver. There wasn't much in me I valued. Without the other half of my equation, suddenly I didn't make sense. I turned my back on the artist in the park, the lover in the bedroom, the whore in the street. Perhaps not completely on the whore in the street—I let that person in me have his way, let him be led along, led by the flesh. A kind of greed commenced to grow in me, a greed of experience, as if the only way you make a lie the truth is by going all the way through it. As if you let something pull you down, all the way to China.

But instead of China, I went out to California.

A day north of New Orleans, I came to a highway that I knew from maps and the TV would take me all the way west. Route 66 was the carpet you rode along until you got to where dreams were made. Anybody could be an actor, anybody could be king. The thing was just getting out there. After Missouri and Arkansas, the road moved back and forth like a rhabdomancer's forked stick, dowsing for the cool moisture just beneath the surface. Something to mitigate the miles and miles of pained, almost guilty heat. Passing through small oil towns in Texas and New Mexico, rolling along under skies that had nothing clean left in them, only a dense web of oil and burning air. Seeing men's faces along the way, faces dirty and grease-stained, chapped lips tucked around brown cigars.

I was riding with a trucker named Cliff, zinging along past curio shops and last-chance gas stations, getting ready for the desert, catching a glimpse of reptile farms, a cardboard jaw stretched open next to the road, wooden stands piled with terra-cotta and white-painted pots, bright blue jewelry, straw hats; crossing the vast flat expanse of rock and sand, a landscape unlike anything I'd ever seen, the horizon shimmering, finally the moon rising above it. Riding along with Cliff, who kept the cab filled with smoke and the smell of licorice, the sound of Ferlin Huskey and Patsy Cline.

"How far you going?" he wanted to know when I stepped up into the cab. I said I was probably going as far as he was. He was big and grizzled, and his eyes when he took off his shades were ringed with pale skin. "I'm taking this load to Cucamunga," he said, and I said that was fine—almost at the end of the 66 trail.

Somewhere in Arizona, after a dozen hours in the truck and my kidneys bouncing and rubbing together like the felt dice jiggling in the window, somewhere flat and purple in the desert dawn, I felt the joys and ills of the summer pass away. I sloughed off James, sloughed off perfidy, guilt, and waste, sloughed off a kind of person I had been and wouldn't be again. This would be me, single me—it seemed I wasn't cut out for life in the plural mode.

I felt the exhilaration of moving cool and anonymous

through the long flat night, thoughts like tumbleweeds and tumbleweeds like thoughts flashing quick and raggedy across the road. I was curled up beside a rough stranger; I was a rough stranger myself. I was on my way to California.

Back in Lillienthal, next door to where the DPs came to stay on Oak Street, lived a family named Rumson—parents, two daughters, and a son. Leilani Rumson was two years older than I, and Dolores and Scott were a few years younger. During junior high school the family had moved from Iowa to California, and the following year, we received a photograph of Leilani, in a white dress buoyed up by crinolines, standing smiling on the lawn of their new home in Burbank. Two things that struck me were the size of the eight-by-ten photo and the transformation of the scrawny squinty-eyed teenager I remembered into the mature big-breasted blonde she had become. The image had a beckoning power—not so much toward the figure in high heels in the foreground as to the land behind her, the soft green lap of California itself.

In those days nobody went east from Iowa; the flat plains tilted in only one direction, and that was toward the Pacific. Even though I'd just been living for three months as many states south as I'd now come west, Louisiana wasn't away from home in the way California was. California was away.

I stepped down from the cab onto the hot gravel of Cucamunga. When I got the Rumsons' number from information, and called it, Mrs Rumson sounded as if she could barely remember Iowa, or barely wanted to. I felt the distance hanging on the line.

Yes, well, Leilani doesn't live here anymore—and we don't take her messages either, she said finally. Her tone was exasperated, dismissive. Whether she placed me or not I couldn't tell; all we had in common was the backyard politeness of small towns. Reluctantly she gave me her daughter's Hollywood number.

Leilani came to meet me driving a 1939 green Packard. She sat in the driver's seat with a carful of young men around her, sandy-haired, freckled, the kind you saw in the newsreels. When she got out of the car she was tall, deeply tanned. We drove down Hollywood Boulevard, through a number of small canyons. I marveled at the enormous palm trees, at the exotic sun-smelling air that flowed over us as we rode along. We came to her house, which sat next to a motel and had a neatly divided lawn. A plump cactus stood in the middle of each half. Inside, the color scheme was turquoise and white. She turned on a Bakelite radio, sat down, and pulled out a cigarette.

"Welcome to the land of the fruits and the nuts," she said.

She inhaled, exhaled, and then gave a big horse laugh.

"Which are you?" she asked.

The first afternoon, the activity didn't stop in Leilani's living room. The boys who'd been with her in the car either looked at me with an intensity I found disconcerting or ignored me altogether. No one was ever without a cigarette; the room was a smoky cloud. The phone would ring, and Leilani would go into the bedroom and talk with whoever it was, and shortly one or another of the sandy-haired men would be scooting out the door. Behind the house was a patio, which seemed to connect with other small bungalows by a series of stone paths. I was disappointed not to see a pool.

One of the intense young men came out to where I was standing on the patio.

"You'll need to cut that hair," he said matter-of-factly. "It's not the look."

I wondered what he meant—films?—and ran my hand back through it, as over the spine of a small endangered animal.

"My name's Chapman White," he announced. He thrust out his hand in a not very successful gesture of spontaneity. I shook it, and told him mine, at which he wrinkled his nose. "That won't do," he said. "Ask Leilani to think up something better for you. She's a whiz at it."

I wondered what Leilani did for a living. She seemed to be well enough off to have a nice car and house. And everybody in her place was helping himself to this and that, drinking and eating. I looked in to where she was sitting on a long low couch, nodding her head and laughing. The TV was on, as well as the radio, and everybody in the room was speaking twice as loud as normal—it seemed as if they were all trying to fill it up with sound, a big square balloon of sound, each vying for the greatest volume.

"So what else does Leilani do, besides giving out new names?" I asked Chapman. I was offhand, natural.

"Ask her," he suggested.

"She is in show business, isn't she?" I was less offhand; this was an important question.

"Oh sure, sure. She's very big in show business just now." He laughed out loud and dropped his cigarette onto the concrete. "You go ahead and ask her all about it." He turned and hurried back inside.

Chapman was good-looking, I thought to myself, but he wasn't in any way attractive. His clean-cut image and the smell of the cologne he wore made him seem slightly fraudulent, as if his wholesome intention had overshot the mark. He was like a replica of what he wanted to project, instead of the thing itself, and this made me distrust him. But I could see that the half-dozen others in the room were largely of the same design: too decorously hearty, too self-aware. Though nothing had been said about my being part of such a crowd, I shrank from the affinity. They were all so well-groomed, predictable; and so white. I was different.

I strolled back inside and sat down at the end of the couch. Leilani moved next to me, and in the hubbub of conversation and laughter asked me what my plans were. I told her I wanted to get a job, and maybe, how could I say it, get into films.

Of course, nothing simpler. She seemed to think I would have an easy time of it.

"I've got lots of friends, and I work as a sort of agent. Putting people together, making connections." As she spoke, she crossed and uncrossed her legs; she was wearing pedal pushers the same color as the couch, and the effect was of the upholstery coming to life.

"And Chappie over there is missing a roommate," she continued. "You can bunk with him if you like. Otherwise there's always the Hollywood YMCA." She looked at me with heightened interest as she made this last suggestion; I gave her no response, though, unwilling to accept either alternative.

"Or you could stay here and sleep on the couch tonight, and decide tomorrow," she suggested after a pause. "But tomorrow you'll have to be out."

The phone rang again, and she got up and went into the bedroom, excusing herself with a wet smile. I thought we would talk about her family, about Lillienthal, when she returned, but when I asked her about her parents she changed the subject, and I knew not to bring them up again. I kept thinking we'd hit on some familiar topic, or memory, but I found nothing that served. We were both too young to have much of a store of nostalgia, and the fact that we'd lived only a few doors apart for those years in Iowa counted, I realized, for nothing at all. But we drank beer, and finally it didn't matter so much that I was a newcomer. Even the odious Chappie grew more sympathetic as it got to be evening. Then it was time to go out.

Leilani again suggested that I sleep there, so I left my bag in her bedroom, and got back into the Packard with her and Chappie and three others, and we drove to a place called the Red Raven.

It was dimly lit in the large front room, and corridors led toward the back. I kept my sunglasses on—I needed the insulation they provided—and this made it even darker. After a few minutes, I lost sight of Leilani, but Chappie and a boy named Dirk kept bobbing up out of the crowd and asking if I was having a good time.

The crowd was diverse, except that very few women

were in the room. I saw Oriental faces and dark Latinos, and men in denim and leather jackets as well as men in sweaters and Peter Pan collars. Once I caught sight of myself in the long mirror behind the bar, and looked away—I saw that I looked not at all out of place.

Chappie was at my elbow, and he was drunk. An older man stood next to him, a man in a jacket and tie, with a large florid face.

"My friend wants to know if you're a beatnik," he stage-whispered into my ear. "I told him they don't have beatniks where you come from, ha ha, but he says that's what you are. . . ."

He was leaning against me, whiskey and Old Spice gathered in a dank stain around him. He appeared weak and unctuous, and the man with him was like a leering yellow-toothed goat. I pushed away from them both and moved toward the back of the long room. There I leaned against the jukebox, took off my sunglasses, tried to relax. A beatnik. What was that? High metallic laughter came from a nearby booth, and the sound made my stomach turn over. I thought of a phrase I'd heard back in Iowa: cake-eater. This was a room full of cake-eaters. What a long way to come, to find myself mired in such a sleazy school of fish.

The look of disgust on my face repelled no one; the passing men looked at me with interest, while I looked only at my own reflection in the polished glass of the Wurlitzer, a reflection that picked up the pastel blues and pinks of its columns, an image soft and cool and bogus.

"Can I buy you a tune?" a face next to mine in the glass asked. It was a tan face when I turned to it, with sandy-colored hair, and the voice was encouragingly masculine. It belonged to a man in his twenties, who like me was wearing blue jeans, a young man who looked . . . normal.

I said sure, and opted for Elvis Presley.

One particular phrase in "Won't You Wear My Ring Around Your Neck" was indistinct enough to make it seem that Elvis was singing *him* instead of *you*: I only know I love (him), and that (he) love(s) me too . . . and it was like a code, a secret message for those who wanted to hear it. When the lyrics came on, I pointed out the phrase to my companion, and he nodded appreciatively, gave me a wide grin. He went to the bar to get more change, came back, and played it again.

My revulsion at the room, my discomfort, gradually faded as we talked about Elvis and his music. Just two guys shooting the breeze. He was surprised but not displeased that this was my first night in Los Angeles. He was from northern California, had been in town for years and years. I told him my name, and he told me his was Gus, short for Augustus. We had a few beers and he mentioned he lived not far away. We joked around and after a while he asked if I'd like to come home with him. He was affable, reassuring, and I could tell he was eager to have sex. He made me think of a boxer dog, short-legged and tense, the way he moved in quick tight gestures, anxious to please.

What was there now to keep me from pleasure? Pleasure was what I was in California for. I looked around for Leilani, but she had blended into the view. Chappie and his pal were sitting in a booth by the door, the red-faced man with them so puffed-up it looked as if he would soon explode. I nodded as we walked past them, and exited the bar under a hail of scorn. Out on the sidewalk the air was cool and the stars were arranged over the palm trees.

We walked a few blocks and turned in at the gate of a small bungalow. I followed Gus through a trellis hung with ivy, and we came around into a backyard. In the middle of the yard, I was thrilled to find a glowing kidney-shaped pool. It was lit from below, and in no time at all, Gus was bringing out something cold and potent to drink, and I was lowering myself down into the tepid water.

Swimming in a big blue pool at night, looking up from the bottom to where the milky green surface collected and broke apart—this was one of the sweeter luxuries of the senses I had anticipated. How important that setting was to me. Companions were secondary, though my new friend was agreeable enough. I felt as if there were room on the California postcard for only one figure, and that figure was myself. Life turned inward, like the silky waves of blue-green water lapping against my soon-to-be suntanned limbs.

I called Leilani the next day, and she told me Chappie had described my going off with Gus. "So you're one of the fruits," she said.

Staunchly, I maintained that I was a bisexual, and she laughed and laughed into the receiver. "Sure you are, honey—you be whatever you want. One way or the other or both at once, it makes no difference to me. But bisexual sounds like you've got two dicks."

When I went with Gus later in the afternoon to pick up my bag, she was sitting out on the patio, sipping a long blue drink.

"Congratulations," she said to Gus. "You got yourself a

fine all-American here. Better treat him right—this is star material." She slapped my behind.

"You keep in touch, now," she called as we got back into Gus's car.

After the first night with Gus, the following days and nights came fast, in a volley of soft explosions. It didn't matter so much that it was Gus I was with, his own individuality didn't signify—he was the California fantasy. Sand from the beach, and the smell and feel of VO5 hair cream, new tastes, new smells, a new me—that's what Gus evoked. After two weeks, he wanted to know if I felt like doing it with other people. I found out I did. He gave me enough money to move into a small apartment in Venice, and gifts—shirts and swimming suits, cologne. I sat out on the tiny deck and listened to the waves, the gulls and pelicans, let the sun and the salt air fill me up. I hardly ever thought of James.

Gus worked at the Disney Studios as an animator, and had any number of friends in the Valley and on the beaches. We went to Muscle Beach and Laguna, watched them ride the waves at Zuma. I wore my new trunks, learned how to flatten myself out on the board, catch the surf.

Gus knew teachers at Cal Tech and the School of Design, and they gave me work modeling for their drawing and painting classes. Fidgety at first, after the first few sessions I quite liked it. Once in a while I modeled at the studio apartment of one or another of these instructors. I went wherever I was sent and approximated David or Laocoon or a dying slave, in twenty-minute spurts in old wooden office buildings gone white in the sun. If I were a student now, I thought, I'd be one of the earnest faces behind the drawing boards—but here I am inspiring art instead of creating it. The one thing felt as good as the other, suddenly.

I listened to the remarks the teachers made to the students, heard their mumbled bits of advice as I strolled on my breaks through the welter of easels. And got the benefit of that advice while being paid for it, all the while thinking myself about as clever as it was possible to be.

One October weekend I accompanied Gus on a trip out to the Valley to see some of his cowboy friends. I thought of Franklin and his days at Ayrmont Scout Ranch, and of going out with Mom and Dad to see him there; I remembered the face of a cowboy who'd given me a drink from his canteen, out on the trail. I tried to picture him bending over me, the way Gus's friend Ray Ellis bent over me, offering me a drink in his own backyard bunkhouse—I parted my lips and let the tepid sweet-smelling water run down my throat. Water turned to beer, memory turned to flesh. Cowboy Ray was solid and unrelenting. Drinking Lucky Lager and feeling the warmth of attention on my skin, I rode out through the flatland behind the ranch, gripping the reins of a tan palomino. I saw myself on another postcard: a romantic figure caught grinning and careless in the sunlight.

I responded to Gus and Ray, and to their friends Winston and Petitford, as if it were my duty, as if such response were what the moment required. The men were all older than I, and they flattered me outrageously, saying I was sure to be the next Tab Hunter. The bunkhouse was hot and smoky during the day, chilly at night, and Ray burned mesquite along with firewood, which gave the fire an exotic sour smell. Ray was from Montana, and loped along like a wolverine; lean and stubble-chinned, he was a real man to get entangled with. Winston and Petitford were from Kansas, were both over six feet, dark and bowlegged and randy as anything. We all rolled around that weekend; sex was an athletic event, done to show off one's skills, one's prowess, a simple act repeated again and again to garner praise and approval, to perfect the instrument.

> Oh I ain't got no use for the women,
> A true one has never been found,
> They'll stick to a man for his winnings,
> When it's gone they'll turn him down . . .

Ray Ellis sang, throwing a sprig of mesquite at the fire. It was an old song with new life in it. I could see they were all as intent on being cowboys as I was. Winston and Petitford, though they called themselves saddle tramps, were actually workers at the Douglas Aircraft plant in town. When Gus told me this later on, I thought of them in greasy blue coveralls, and my ardor cooled. But they were intense in their bunks—they always kept their boots on, whatever else they wore. And I did, too, that weekend. We were all hoofed animals, naked and sweating and smelling of tobacco. Drunk and boisterous, riding each other home.

Back in town, I kept the Stetson they had given me, and wore it everywhere I went, buying vegetables in the Farmers' Market, going to a movie in Westwood. I wasn't interested in being the Hollywood fantasy now as much as being the cowboy fantasy—the Hollywood fantasy wasn't enough to hold on to. I wanted to be an actor, but I wanted to be an actor playing a cowboy.

I was scornful of Chappie and the other boys who hung around Leilani's; I thought of them as the false fronts of the buildings I'd seen at the Burbank studios. I was sure, however, that I was the authentic article. I kept reinventing myself. I wanted to burn my skin black in the sun; I told people I was half black, or half Indian, and I never mentioned Iowa.

One afternoon a middle-aged man followed me home from the Venice Piggly-Wiggly. When I stopped at the gate and asked him what he wanted, he said it surely was a fine day for a spanking. I was abashed at his directness. He quickly asked if I wanted to earn a fast twenty dollars. My vanity got engaged, and I let him step inside; I said my wife would be home any minute, and for him to hurry up. He took out a Ping-Pong paddle from his back pocket and positioned himself efficiently over my knees. I swatted him (he called me Daddy, and the impropriety angered me enough to swat him harder—he was clearly twice my age), and he came. I think I was appalled by the mechanics of his perversion; I know I felt a surge of vindication when I took his twenty dollars and sent him away.

Being paid for it, I saw, was a glorification of events. I realized that what was otherwise shabby was made right by profit, that sexual capitalism was an enterprising step for any young man to take. Money acted as a spotlight; things fell into place.

With Gus, doing more than one thing at a time was the rule. As if we all had to make up for that unspent time. He had a pair of stereo earphones—it was 1960, and such things were new and wonderful—and he loved having me take him beside the pool while he was wearing them. He would lean back farther and farther, overloading the senses.

Between Gus and Leilani, I learned about reefer and hallucinogenic morning glory seeds (Heavenly Blue and Pearly Gates White were the right shades). Playing around with decadence, I prided myself on trying life, grabbing at this or that in the name of art, or, if not art, experience. Nothing would show on my skin—whatever untoward acts I engaged in would quickly fade, even as my Regalia scar was fading.

Everyone I met in Los Angeles smoked dope or took pills. Everyone was getting away with something. And nothing was permanent.

I read in *Confidential* about a pajama party Tab Hunter had allegedly attended. It was an all-male party; the accompanying photographs were blurred black-and-white shots of young men holding up pillows in front of their faces—all you could really see was their flattops sticking up behind them. The tone of the article was snide, hand-on-hip; the real world was clearly not ready for all-male pajama parties.

Masculinity was hierarchical; actors and hustlers were talked about in different tones of voice. The division got down to those who did it for money, and were therefore vestigially straight, and those who did it because they wanted to. Role models were everywhere. One well-known stud was from Texas and only did it for money; the story was that at certain high-toned parties he stirred the punch with his joint. He had a muscular inflated body, with tattoos crawling up his arms; he was always in demand. Nobody wanted him to do it because he wanted to.

Everybody worked on technique. I struck tough macho poses in the bars, and found I liked the Raven better each time I went there. We were all one another's audience. I took the same stance on the modeling stand in art classes and off; my hair was long in front and fell forward over my forehead, like Edd Cookie Byrnes's, Gus and his friends said. I was dark from the time spent on the beaches, from the hours spent beside the pools of all my new friends.

Leilani took me one night to call on an old buddy of hers who worked as a female impersonator: Mel or Melba, depending on the hour. Leilani had a new friend, Billy, whom she also brought along; we were meant to be a diverse group. Billy was somewhat different from the clean-cut young men she usually liked—he was lean and countrified, with a big hayseed grin and a long pink dick he called Clyde. "Clyde don't go in for none of that," he'd say. Or "Me and Clyde had a *real* good time."

Billy took too many drugs that night, and sat on a chair next to the bed while Leilani and the impersonator and I addressed each other on it. We laughed that Clyde remained upright, like the marker on a grave, while Billy nodded off; finally Leilani pulled Billy into the kitchen and splashed him with cold water from the tap. The impersonator still wore small flecks of sequins from the night's performance; they dotted his eyebrows, the side of his neck. I thought how much he resembled a swan, the way he moved through the air, cutting it, then slowing, plumping himself out.

With just the two of us there in the bedroom, I tried to be active and attentive, but I couldn't keep an erection. Mel plied me with compliments and no little expertise, but it was no good. After a few moments of the particular awkwardness such a situation engenders, he sighed and said, "Turn over. You're too tentative. You mustn't ever be tentative."

"I'm sorry," I replied, and then he was on top of me and riding away like some western stud. And I was thrilled and mortified at the same time.

Afterward, lying on the bed and watching him dress—putting on the dress and the heels, he was like a caterpillar becoming a butterfly, or vice versa—I couldn't get over life's perversity. Instead of feeling ashamed for taking it from such a sissy-icon, I felt fabulous. "So long, sweetie," he said and kissed me on the cheek when we left.

Sex was everywhere. The men who handled the vegetables in the outdoor markets, the bus conductors crossing back and forth over the wide grid of the city, baking in their seats. The midwesterners, the men from Oregon, the sailors—so many young men in white hanging around the corners of the frame. So many arms and legs pending, only waiting to engage, to be engaged.

Any new situation would do. My body was like one of those shiny California convertibles I saw on Sunset and La Brea, and I cruised around in it with ill-concealed pride.

The scar on my stomach faded away; I was advised to use cocoa-butter and Vitamin E. At first I'd elaborated on it with various melodramatic tales. Nothing seemed good enough as it was; the state of California was all invention. My morality took a turn for the earth, and I let it sag downward. Immorality wasn't it, exactly—I never stole from anyone or did anyone harm. My relationship with Gus was free and loose—he didn't seem to want me to be in any way monogamous. He liked seeing me with other men, as out on the ranch with Ray and the cowboys. Monogamy had seemed to me a natural law when I was growing up, but out here in the land of opportunity, relationships weren't the point, relations were.

Those months in California were a sweet bafflement to me. That you could be with someone and yet not be with him, that you could couple with whoever struck your fancy and not feel guilty—this was fuel for the spirit. Nobody was ever betrayed, because the ground rules didn't include fidelity. You let your emotions flap in the breeze.

❖

LIFE DRAWING

I managed to get to the Hollywood YMCA for a workout once or twice a week. John Saxon swam in the yellow-tiled pool there—at least everyone said he did, but I seemed always to have just missed him. There was no shortage of other thespians about, groaning at the lat machine or oiling their already oily flesh in the steam room. Middle-aged men vocalized in the shower, and younger types scowled and preened in various stages of undress. Steam clung to the walls; the moisture in the air gave all sounds an added resonance.

Smaller exercise rooms off the large gymnasium were always in use. It was in one of these that I first glimpsed a peculiar group of half a dozen men who were silently and purposefully going through a series of wrestling moves. Peculiar, because they were all but one of them not over four feet tall—midgets, short thick-muscled gents with heavy square jaws and bowed legs. Grunts and the impact of flesh slapping flesh were the only sounds they produced. They seemed to communicate in a kind of sign language, and it was an exceedingly odd thing to witness.

At the center of the group stood a man of normal dimensions. He looked Asian or American Indian, and was powerful and sinewy. His chest and shoulders were bare, and the muscles of his upper body were exaggerated, gleaming with sweat. He would point to one, then another of the smaller men, and each would turn and produce a move, half somersault, half takedown, and look back to him for approval. It was hard to guess the age of the midgets, but he looked to be in his mid-thirties.

One of the midgets was leaning over with his hands pressed against the mat, and grinned at me as I stood watching. He had irregular teeth and stubble on his chin,

109

but his eyes were the eyes of a child. Standing there in the doorway, I felt I was watching a silent film with just the thump-thump of arms and legs hitting the mat, and the sharp smell of their bodies.

Abruptly, the activity ceased, and after a sign from the big man the athletes filed one by one out of the room. Now as they passed they all smiled up at me—they seemed to be glad of an audience, however small.

I stepped into the room to let them pass, and the big man looked at me directly for the first time. His face was sinister but attractive, lean with high cheekbones, and light discerning eyes. A thin mustache, long hair a shade or two darker tied back with a rubber band. He didn't smile, but showed his teeth, and as he looked me full in the face I felt that familiar welcome heat. The veins on his forearms stood out; his chest was damp from his exertions. His look was ninety-nine percent threatening perhaps—but I only saw the remaining one percent.

"Okay," he said, "what's up, boy?" He spoke softly, just a turn up from the previous silence, in nearly a whisper.

"What's *up*?"

The threat in his voice wasn't a real threat either, I decided. I was happy to presume that all men I met might be sympathetic.

"I used to wrestle—in high school," I said, as if that explained my interest.

"Can't be that long ago." He stepped closer to me, then reached out and put his hands on my shoulders and squeezed the flesh, then moved to my chest and did the same there. His hands were calloused, and cool. Instead of drawing back from him, I stood up straight, enduring his rough inspection. As if, as if—I didn't know what.

After a moment, I grew embarrassed that this rough stranger was manhandling me, and that I was letting him. He was looking full into my eyes, and his lips were pulled back in the half smile, half grimace that I'd seen as he directed the wrestlers.

"About a hundred and sixty-five pounds, I'd say. You could use a little more meat. If you were mine, I'd put some muscle here, and here." His hands moved over me, quick and mean and electric.

Finally he let me go, and I let out the breath I hadn't realized I'd been holding. I took a little step to catch my balance, and he stepped back.

"Anyway, I don't handle full-size competitors. Just the shorts: weekends at the Garden and the Coliseum." He reached into the pocket of his sweatpants and pulled out some pink pieces of paper, tickets, fliers.

"That's me," he said, pointing to a name on the wrinkled flier, halfway down the page:

WHITTAKER LEE PRESENTS:
RAGTIME COWBOY JOE vs. LITTLE SAMSON
Half-Pint Action that packs a Gallon Punch!!
Preliminaries 3 PM   Main Event 5 PM

"You come and see the show. The shorts are the first act on the bill."

He nodded his head, as if I'd replied, as if I'd said something agreeable, and turning from me left the room.

❖

That Saturday, of course, I had to show up at the Coliseum. Leilani came with me, wearing a big white hat and a flowered dress. She was overdressed, and knew it, and didn't mind—as we found our seats in the milling crowd, she tossed her head back and forth, excited by the roughness in the air. She was thrilled she didn't see anyone she knew, pointed out various handsome possibilities ringside, required soft drinks and popcorn, and finally two hot dogs.

We sat in the third row as the midget match was about to begin. Over the loudspeaker, Ragtime Cowboy Joe's theme music started up, tinny and scratchy, the voices of the Andrews Sisters grown thin and frazzled from overplaying. The crowd sang and hooted along with the music, and one of the tiny athletes I'd seen at the Y came scurrying up the aisle. He wore a big black hat and a black-and-white fringed jacket and tights, and pulled out two shiny revolvers as he climbed up into the ring. He fired his caps, then reholstered the guns and ran around the ring waving his hat in the air. The crowd screamed with pleasure and anticipation—he was clearly a favorite.

Little Samson got no such musical fanfare; he appeared at the opposite corner of the ring from Joe, wearing an animal skin that sent Leilani into spasms of laughter next to me. "What is that?" she screamed. *"Cat?"* The people around us screamed, too; Samson looked chagrined, and I hoped he wouldn't recognize me just then, but soon the two were running at each other in the middle of the ring, running in and poking and tearing at each other's head and shoulders.

At first Little Samson seemed to be getting the better of it—he put Cowboy Joe into a quick pinning combination—but Joe kicked up out of it before he was against the mat, and then the two mixed it up pretty evenly. They were so small that once they were down on the mat it was hard to see them; the crowd was on its feet all through the match. Little Samson stuck his fingers in Joe's eye, and Joe retaliated by taking a bite out of his other hand. It looked like the real thing for a few minutes, but that abated. Finally, Samson sat on his opponent's back after taking him to the mat with a flying mare, and turned him over with one deft motion, pressed him down, and took the pin.

It had happened too fast for the crowd—they were indignant and squawked their displeasure. The favorite had lost, and too fast. Now the two chased each other back and forth around the ring, the crowd clamoring, and Whittaker jumped up into the ring, dressed in tight white pants, T-shirt, and shiny leather boots, and grabbed the winner and hoisted him up on his shoulder. He stood there in the center with the spotlight bouncing off them, and the clamoring changed to cheers.

"Oh my God," shouted Leilani. "I'm *exhausted*!"

I watched Whittaker carry Little Samson down the aisle. Programs and soda cups rained through the air as they passed; Cowboy Joe followed ingloriously a few minutes later. As had been agreed upon beforehand, Leilani stayed for the main event, and I went back to the dressing rooms to find my new friend and his charges.

When I pushed open the door, I saw the two wrestlers laughing and signing happily to each other. They looked up quizzically at my entrance, but Whittaker came out from behind the screen and I shook his hand, and then the hands of the combatants, and everyone was quite flushed and excited. I watched as the men stripped off their trunks and tights and headed for the shower. Cowboy Joe had a big dark joint that fairly fell out of his trunks—the size and color were a shock; he must have had it wrapped tight under his jock in the ring. Little Samson was demure, and grabbed a towel. The two men ran into the shower room, giggling like schoolgirls.

"Don't you two be pissing on each other in the shower now!" yelled Whittaker after them, laughing and giving me a wink. I gathered from their high spirits that the bout had been a success, as such things were measured. It wasn't really wrestling, I thought to myself, remembering my own valiant bouts back in Lillienthal, but it was something.

Whittaker picked up Cowboy Joe's sporting records, and we left the stadium as the main match got underway. Waves of catcalls and applause spread out and receded around us as the full-size gladiators had at one another. Whittaker drove an old maroon Ford convertible, and his long hair flew out behind him as we sped along. He lived not far from where I did in Venice, on a houseboat, and after we'd dropped off Samson and Joe at their favorite miniature golf course—a reward round for a bout well played, as was the custom—he took me home with him.

Although it was still daylight out, and the air smelled of sunshine and mackerel, inside the low rocking houseboat it felt like nighttime. Two rooms and a sort of kitchen, sort of bath, all of it dark and musty, and lights that were draped with scarves. He lit a stick of incense and gave me a can of beer. The label was Primo; it was a Hawaiian beer he liked to drink that reminded him of home. Home was the island of Oahu; he told me he was a "haopa haole," half Caucasian and half Chinese-Hawaiian, and that he'd left the islands ten years before. But he missed Oahu, and would have liked to go back, only there had been some trouble, something with the police, something murky, not his fault.

As he told me bits and pieces of his story, he rolled a joint, bigger and fatter than I usually ingested. The grass was potent, and he sat back on his heels, rocked slowly back and forth like a man in a trance.

"This will get you to your true nature," he said softly, regarding me through narrowed eyes the wispy chain of smoke.

The smoke filled my lungs, and made me self-conscious—that is, it kept me mute. Sometimes all you can do is breathe in and out, forget about talk entirely. Whittaker's loquaciousness faded, too. He sat there in the half-light, silent as an idol. When the joint was finished, he shook his head and gave a little laugh, his voice thin and raspy, and put his finger to his lips. The outer silence seemed to cover an inner soliloquy. Who was he agreeing and disagreeing with?

Whittaker's eyes widened, and he kept his finger to his lips as he crawled across the floor toward me. Then, as he had in the gym, he put his hands on my chest, gently at first, then less gently, kneading my flesh, reaching under my shirt and pulling hard on my nipples, smiling fiercely all the while. With the grass, what pain I might have felt was merely another form of pleasure. His intensity had me breathing hard, stiffening in my trousers; unseen companions leaned over his shoulder. As he roughly pulled off my clothes, I felt there were other bodies in the room, pressed against us, erotic phantoms all under his charge.

Rough and gentle, gentle and rough, he was relentless.

He kept his own clothes on while stripping me of mine. As I lay flat against the floor, I could feel the motion of the water moving beneath us, and I arched my back and stretched upward as if I were floating on the wave. No music, no words—the only sound was the creaking of the lines outside, the steady lapping of the current underneath us. How many hands he seemed to have, and then his mouth, warm and firm, everywhere at once. Each time I moved to respond to his touch with my own, he pushed me back down, kept me flat against the boards. It was sex as I'd never had it, and the pleasure of unmitigated passivity was profound.

I let Whittaker and his phantoms have their way with me, let the sharp points of his touch burst again and again against my flesh.

Finally, he was astride my chest, breathing heavily, and in a series of impatient moves was standing up and pulling off his pants, scowling now, angry at the sudden immediacy—letting his joint swing free of the white fabric, letting me see the intricate tattoo that stretched across his hip, a blue-and-red serpent, all glittering meticulous scales against his tawny flesh. A serpent that pushed its head into his groin, into the short curly hair there: the one snake swallowing another, the long smooth trunk of skin jutting out from the creature's wide-open blue mouth. Jutting out like the fist of an army recruitment poster—wanting *you!*—jutting out thick and hard and wet at the tip. The explosion, the tempest arriving all at once, the rain splashing down, hot white rain and the smell of tar and vermouth full in the face, a storm I wanted never to end.

His high dry laugh covered it all. Then the serpent recoiling, with the night all around us, and finally, sleep.

The next morning I felt queasy, and all through the week following I bore the consequences of my coupling: a dulcet ache, centered on small circular islands of bruised flesh. The first few days, I was perplexed, then by midweek I was ready to see Whittaker again; when he called on Friday I was both anxious and euphoric. Gus came by on Friday night, but I put him off—the sex we'd had together now seemed bland, hardly worth the effort. Gus was a sweet guy, but sweetness had no premium.

When I did see Whittaker again, after the Saturday match, he announced he was going to introduce me to a friend of his, a photographer. "Never hurts to have some good beefcake around," he said. "Marion does a nice job. People always like to see photographs, don't they?"

I supposed it was good for my career. We picked up Cowboy Joe, who that afternoon hadn't wrestled on the Coliseum bill, and who seemed out of sorts. He was dressed in a blue-and-white seersucker suit, with gold-rimmed sunglasses bridging his nose; he climbed into the backseat of the Ford without so much as a nod of greeting, and he kept on a constant scowl as we drove along.

The fattest man I'd ever seen opened the door of a blue-

and-yellow frame bungalow on Doheny Boulevard, and we entered a large cluttered studio.

"How do, Mr Lee. How do, Joe. And who is this young specimen? How *do*! Marion Sykes, at your service."

His hands were hot as he pressed mine in greeting, and bits of silver fillings sparkled in his smile. He had red frizzy hair, and his skin was smooth. Large lamps were here and there illumined, and the voice of Judy Garland came blazing out of a record console.

"Um-humm-hum," the photographer hummed along, moving expertly and decorously among the lights and wires.

"Take off your clothes," Whittaker instructed me, and gave me a can of beer. Joe settled into a big plush arm-chair, swinging his feet slowly back and forth. The photographer brought Joe a beer, too, cajoling him softly, giving him some magazines to read, very solicitous.

He turned back to me. "If you're shy, you can change in the bathroom."

As I entered that room, his voice became high and affable. "There's a robe hanging on the door."

I slid out of my jeans and sat on the stool pulling off my boots. There were a number of signed photographs on the walls, bright flattopped young men smiling earnestly. When I turned on the light by the mirror, roaches ran across the sink.

I pulled on the robe and came back out into the larger room. Marion was holding what looked to be a slingshot, and said I should put it on. It was a posing strap, a flimsy contraption that got adjusted and readjusted. I had seen photos of men in these straps before, in magazines that Gus had from such places as Athletic Models Guild.

Pleased to contemplate my own photo among theirs, I moved to stand in front of a sheet of gray paper unrolled against the wall. Whittaker rubbed oil on my shoulders and back, and had me do a set of push-ups for tone. When it seemed I was ready, Marion began shooting. He stopped once or twice, saying to Whittaker, "He's showing," and then Whittaker would readjust the strap until I was again sufficiently covered.

The lights were warm, and I struck those poses I'd been taught to hold in art classes. I was very much enjoying the whole endeavor when Marion said, "Let's do some special shots now," and I was instructed to step out of the strap and to stand there as God had made me.

"Nobody will see these," Marion assured me. "These are only for my own private stock. And this is for your trouble," he said, and reached into his pocket and pulled out a twenty-dollar bill. He shot another roll with Whittaker smiling and nodding behind him as I crouched and stretched and grinned.

Marion never touched me, for which I was grateful—his pale hands stroked the air but didn't touch me. He rolled around his studio like a boulder of flesh, a dripping glacier. It wasn't the cameraman that signified, but the camera. Casting things in this detached fashion, I was able to relax. The grotesqueness of the situation had nothing to do with me.

At the end of the session I was exhausted. Immortality is always hard work. The agreement was that I was to receive a half-dozen prints for myself—two head shots and the rest body shots in the posing strap. The later, unencumbered, prints, I was again assured, no one else would ever see.

I dressed. Cowboy Joe had had a few beers, but I noticed they hadn't made him any more agreeable. He sat scowling in the armchair, and only nodded his head at me slightly when we left. He ignored Whittaker's goodbye completely. I didn't envy him being left alone with Marion.

But presently I was back on the houseboat and it was evening again. Whittaker was giving me another joint to smoke, and I was again at the mercy of the Pacific current, rocking back and forth with the salty tide.

It was the middle of the night when I woke to the sound of someone knocking slowly and persistently at the door. Whittaker, a lighter sleeper than I, was out of the bed beside me before I was half awake; he wrapped a length of flowered cloth around his waist as he crossed the room, and after a mumbled exchange through the door, he opened it.

He signaled to whoever it was standing there to be quiet, and pointed back in my direction. More mumbling; I heard words that sounded like fish, in fact were fish: mahimahi and pompano, hake . . . quick glittering images that splashed through my sleep. Then they crossed the room and disappeared into the kitchen. I heard the large freezer door being opened, and further consultation, soft laughter.

"A little late in the day for mahimahi," Whittaker said, his thin amused voice just carrying into the bedroom.

The freezer door closed, and the visitor crept past me and out the door, clutching a package wrapped in tinfoil. Whittaker came back to bed, and I kept my eyes closed, feigning sleep. He threw his arm across me, and a fish smell was on his fingers, a smell that bled softly and innocuously into my dreams.

In the morning I asked who the visitor had been, and Whittaker replied, "No one you know."

"Something about fish," I persisted.

He looked at me, made a quick decision, and shrugged his shoulders. "Mahimahi," he said, pronouncing it "my, my," as if commenting on my nosiness. Then, off-handedly, he said, "I . . . we supply a few local restaurants with rare fish from the islands. Frozen, of course."

"Of course. But why in the middle of the night?"

He smiled. "Why not? It's cooler."

And safer, I thought. "What's in the fish, Whittaker?"

"Oh, nothing special. A little opium in some of them."

"A little opium."

He smiled his squint-smile. "How do you think I can afford to keep the *Queen Mary* here?" He indicated the creaking houseboat. "Nothing serious," he went on. "But you know, midget wrestlers wouldn't keep you in suntan oil."

I wanted to say I didn't expect them to; that I hoped such goings-on would have nothing to do with me. I wondered what Mom and Dad would say if they knew there was opium in the freezer—let alone the police.

Opium was a subject too large, too exotic for me, and at the first opportunity I brought it up with Leilani. In numerous ways she had always shown me how inexperienced and naive I was; here I thought she might protect me from things I did not understand, which is what she did.

Immediately she gave me one of her big horse laughs, a laugh that allowed for everything but surprise. "That's *your* Whittaker? My God, people are enterprising! Perhaps I judged him and his little friends too quickly. . . . Opium in the fish," she mused. "Your friend wants to get ahead, but judging from the talk in Venice, I would say he should cut bait and get out of there."

"How do you know these things?" I asked.

"Mother simply knows," she said seriously.

The next Saturday afternoon she went with me again to the match, and afterward came back to the dressing rooms.

"Pussy on the gunnel!" someone yelled out from one of the tiny rooms as we moved down the long corridor.

"You bet!" Leilani shouted back.

In the sweaty dressing room Whittaker was glum, Leilani cool and flowery. The midgets were sent to the showers with the usual admonitions, and Leilani, to my horror, perched herself on the edge of the changing table and said, "What's with the opium, Whittaker? Are you mad?"

Whittaker was immediately furious. He powered himself up like an engine, called me a traitor, and told us both to get out. "Never trust a goddam haole!" he cried.

But Leilani was unimpressed and stood her ground. "Look," she said, interrupting him, hands on hips. "You're not the only one packing fish around here. Mickey did you a big favor bringing me into this. It's not the safest business in the world, you know. You have competitors. You even, my dear, have a few enemies."

He looked at her disdainfully. "You're crazy. No one knows about this."

"No, of course not," she replied sarcastically. "All the junkies keep it a secret because they like fish."

"And what do you know about it?"

"I have connections," Leilani replied calmly. "There has been talk."

Whittaker looked from one of us to the other. "Talk?"

"High-grade opium in small quantities every other Wednesday, coming from a houseboat in Venice. Sound familiar?"

"Jesus!" Whittaker exclaimed. "People are such shits!"

"That they are, honey," Leilani said, touching her hair.

When Whittaker had calmed down he asked her what he should do, having decided to trust her, I think, as much because of her calm cynicism as for the information she brought. For my part, I was amazed that Lillienthal should have produced the two of us within the same era—Leilani, who would have not been intimidated by an ax murderer, and me, so intimidated by Leilani. But then I was Lillienthal's rule, not Leilani.

"First of all," she replied, "find yourself another scam. You're not cut out for drug-running. Few of us are. Time for a change. And get rid of whatever you have in the way of . . . stock."

"That's it?"

"Just do it. And don't be cute about saving something for a rainy day. If they come they'll bring the dogs." She looked at me. "And in the meantime, consider this a gift from the Mick here." She smiled at me.

But apparently Whittaker didn't do what he was supposed to do, or he missed one of the fish in the freezer, or something was planted there, because the police took him away, and seized the houseboat, and Whittaker went to jail. I never saw him again, and never knew what happened to him in the end.

❖

Toward spring, Leilani finally told me of a friend of hers at Paramount Studios who was looking for young men for a surfing movie. I rubbed on a layer of cocoa butter and went in to see him.

His office was on the second lot, and I was enthralled as I passed the pink-costumed dancers and the moving property. This was the world for me. Another young man sat in the producer's office, with a bottle of Coke in his fist. He sat looking at me with a half-scowl as I answered Mr Cherry's questions. It was a fight scene that he wanted us to improvise. He told us both to take off our shirts. I didn't have any trunks with me? That was all right, I could do it in my undershorts. He came out from behind his desk, eating an apple as he talked, and watched us as we rolled around on the carpet.

The other boy was stronger, but I was the better wrestler. I was thinking how pleased Coach Mannucci would have been to see me throwing a whizzer with such finesse when my opponent reached down and grabbed hold of my crotch. Mr Cherry said, "Take him, Chet," and in my confusion I let myself be turned and flattened. "Take him," he said again, his voice higher.

The apple fell to the floor and I saw him undoing his fly, while the boy on top of me spat on his hand and wedged it up between my legs, under my cotton briefs. Then I felt him up against my backside, and Mr Cherry pounding away, standing over us. I struggled to get up, and then figured what the hell, and the scene got played out in a series of quick hard strokes.

I didn't know how to behave afterward. I couldn't think of a word to say, and anyway the look on Cherry's face as he buckled up again was so unpleasant that conversation seemed a dim idea. Things were moving too fast for me. There hadn't been time for it to be sexy—all I felt was dislocation. The other boy, Chet, offered me a cigarette, while Cherry talked on the phone.

Chet said, "Don't worry about it. They'll give you something."

"But I'm an actor," I said.

"Sure, sure," he said, grinning, and he seemed suddenly far older than Cherry.

Chet was fair-skinned when you looked close. He pulled on his pants indifferently, letting the ash from the cigarette he was smoking fall to the floor. He let the smoke come out around his teeth, then he blew out a long puffy O. His was a face in the newsreels, the Times Square smoker one saw on TV every New Year's Eve, pale and remote. He might never have pinned me to the carpet.

He told me he had done a few pictures for this producer, Cherry. He let me know he had been around. "You do what they want you to and pretty soon they put you in a real feature," he explained.

I asked him what feature he was doing, and he gave me a look of cool contempt.

"I wouldn't be doing this," he said, indicating with a shrug all that had happened, "if I was in a *feature*."

He grinned, and I saw that the old man in him was a handsome old man, conniving and imagining, putting one over on fate.

"Once you're established, you see, you only do other features. And my acting coach says that whenever they get ready for me, I'll be ready for them. What do you think?"

He turned to me, edging down over his forehead a hat not unlike the one I had, sticking his thumbs out from the belt loops at his waist. He made me think of James Cagney, all strut and bravado.

I said I thought he'd make it, but, meanwhile, what about me and my career?

Deflated, obliged to regard me, he said, "You'll be all right. Your nose is too short, maybe. But they can fix that."

Just then the producer hung up the phone and came around his desk.

"Okay now, boys," he announced. "It's all settled. We're about to go out to the beach to start filming another cinematic masterpiece! It'll put you boys on the map! Give you something to write home about!"

He stood between us, beaming broadly.

"I always like to do my boys a favor—ain't I just Father Flanagan?"

He clapped his hands together, filled with the enthusiasm of the moment, and grabbed us both by our joints. The smoke in Chet's face obscured his smile.

❖

Two days later, Mr Cherry's secretary called. She said filming had already begun, and that my scene was to be shot the next day. Chet was not mentioned. This was fine with me: it was easy to pretend that nothing sexual had occurred. Besides, once you were in show business, it didn't matter how you'd got there.

They sent a car for me just after sunrise. Near Luna Beach, a stretch of sand was roped off, with trailers and cars parked out around it like wagons. At the center of the heat Mr Cherry was angling through the surf like a crab in blue and khaki. He saw me and waved me over to a woman sitting behind a card table. She gave me my lines, marked in yellow, out of a script titled *Surf Holiday*. The movie followed a group of fraternity boys pursuing sorority girls at spring break. My costume was a pair of surfing trunks and a necklace of coral beads. I was to learn my lines and wait for my scene. Any fool could do it, said the yellow-haired man who, in the makeup tent, slapped Texas Dirt all over me. Outside, in the back of a truck, men were playing hearts, swearing loudly and copiously at every hand.

The blue Pacific lay before me, calm and reassuring.

Everyone was dressed more or less the same, and this made it difficult to tell who was an actor and who wasn't. I watched a handsome well-built man with a beard as he stood at the table where there were kegs of water and fruit punch. I was wondering if this was a star I should know when he walked back across the sand and picked up a boom and held it over the patch on the strand where Mr Cherry was working. The sun blazed down, and I felt the Texas Dirt running down my sides. I got into the shade of a fat palm tree, and drank a cup of fruit punch, and waited for my career to begin.

Finally, Cherry came over. He was accompanied by another man, who frowned at me from behind his tinted sunglasses.

"He'll have to get a haircut," he said, and Cherry nodded his head vigorously, clapped me on the shoulder.

"No problem there, is there, Mick?" he asked. I said there wasn't, and soon I was sitting back in the makeup tent, with the dark pelt I had worked so hard at curling beneath me on the sand.

Crew-cut once again, I returned to the beach.

Cherry took me by the arm, and we walked back and forth on the wet sand.

"You have your lines, right?"

I said I did, and then went through them. In fact, there were only six of them, two to be shot that day. He was satisfied by my breathless recitation, and nodded his head.

We walked back to the circle of cameras and camp chairs.

"Just be yourself," he said.

I was placed next to two girls in bikinis and one young man in trunks like mine. They looked at me, and we shook hands, and waited while the lights were set.

Then the man came up and snapped a chalkboard, and a voice called, "Action."

And that was when I knew my affliction. The girl said her line, which was my cue. And I was dumb.

My body was seized by a kind of phobia, something

that manifests itself under light, when the great camera swings toward one: a galloping frenzied paucity.

I was catatonic.

We tried it once, and we tried it twice. The other young actors looked at me with contempt. All I could do was grin idiotically, unable to say a word.

The lines fell in on me, crushed me.

I was led away.

In the first-aid tent, they took away my costume. I lay on a cot, let a damp cloth cover my eyes. I saw what the camera never saw: my performance. I was the glorious film actor of the decade, revealed in a few quick scenes. I was dashing, swashbuckling. Assurance was everywhere I moved, and my voice was like a rippling flag over the audience. I dreamed the audience, dreamed their adoration, their applause.

And then the same car that had brought me out brought me back home, and I had to realize that I was nothing but a fool.

❖

To realize one's a fool at the age of eighteen is better, no doubt, than coming to that realization at twenty-eight or thirty-eight. Still, I felt self-awareness whip through me like an icy wind, snapping off the blossoms of my ego. I felt my pretensions emptied out of me, and with them the idea of myself as a movie star. On the beach, I'd endured a shot of staggering humility; I wasn't an actor, nor was it possible I would ever become one. Something fundamental was missing. My flesh had got ahead of my spirit, that was all. And it wasn't only my incapacity on the set, it was all that had led me to it. My determined profligacy in the last few months rebounded on me, and left me numb. Now I was one person in need of another. Now I was in flight from myself.

I didn't bother to tell Leilani I was done with my career, and there wasn't anyone else to tell. Gus and I had stopped running around together. Whittaker was in jail. There was no present to put my finger on; the current moment was unendurable. And the past, as it will, came flooding back.

Gradually, but with a needful intensity, I came to focus again on the image of James. This was someone who had believed in me. I thought of our nights on Borchardt Street, of the last time I had seen him, stretched out in the moonlight. The impulse to come to California, to show the world that I was something special, had leaped out of the ashes of my relationship with him, and my betrayal.

I didn't realize, hadn't realized, that the best part of myself was still in New Orleans. Finally, I saw that someone strong and loving, someone who'd urged me to make something of myself, was a gift, a gift I had thrown away. I knew that all the dogging around I'd done since hadn't gotten me any closer to being the man I wanted to be—I had pretended to be a creature sleek and impervious, but I was a pitiably long way from being sophisticated. Whatever was special about my affair with James didn't have to do with the men who had come after him; nothing special about the small change of random sex, nothing special about using sex to be a movie star. I saw myself for the thick-skinned jumped-up nobody I was. Common as muck, suddenly, with nothing of my own to sustain me, only a great white empty echo.

The waves of the Pacific rolled in, and gulls wheeled through the air. How quickly things ended, how abruptly and how cruelly. James James James—I picked up his name and put it on like a bright stone around my neck. And the power of the love I'd felt for him, and done my best to ignore, returned. I determined to go back to New Orleans and to find him. Once there, I'd convince him that I was at last a serious person. I would be worthy of his affection again, if only he'd give me another chance. My months in California were the fantasy, he was the reality. I needed him.

A bus took me back across the desert, back through Barstow and Albuquerque, over the flatlands of Arizona and Texas. I slept and dreamed, felt myself rolled backward like a strip of film. As if time could be erased, as if one's actions were only smudges of charcoal on a pad. I moved backward like one of those cartoon figures on Gus's desk: a stick figure in a comic-book life.

But James wasn't in New Orleans. Mrs Odum said he'd gone north after Christmas; she didn't know why. Obliging as ever, she asked if I'd be wanting to move back into my room. The last I saw of Mrs Odum she was standing in the parlor, the boarders behind her glum and sleek as crows.

On the dock at Decatur, watching the old boats and the new boats passing, I got back some resolve. The smell of salt water and tar, the freighters up from Veracruz and Brownsville, all the coming and going of life sounded in the bells and the horns. I had a friend and I'd lost him. It was time to go back home. I was a young man, with a young man's strength, and I would find a way to reclaim my purpose. The river flowed south, but I had to go north.

I hitchhiked up through Louisiana, following the highway over Lake Ponchartrain, up past Vicksburg, along the Arkansas border into Missouri. At intervals along the road, the river would appear in the near distance, under the moon shining flat and milky, or by daylight a turgid stretch of brown. What a massive glory it was; the turpentine pines and scrub would swallow the view, or rain would streak the windshield, but the pieces of it were soothing, a familiar calm.

Two days north, I was passing through Byron County, Illinois, when I was picked up by two teenage revelers in a rusty old Dodge truck. It was the weekend, and they were set to stay drunk all through it. We weaved back and forth along the highway, pulling on a bottle of whiskey. When the local police waved us over, I was on my way to being as drunk as the two of them.

I was booked on a vagrancy charge, after self-righteously defending myself to the local sheriff, who had been rousted out of bed to deal with us. The two locals were remanded to their parents, but I was put in the county jail for the night, thrown into a large holding cell with my jacket for a pillow and half a dozen snoring wine-stained men for company.

The glow from the alcohol faded soon enough, and the light of day when it came was as cruel as I had yet seen or felt it. The grainy blue-gray light gathered around the sleeping forms of the men on the floor and on the ledge along the wall. The smell of urine and cheap wine and clothes as old as the jail itself seemed to grow stronger as the light found them, and I smelled my fingers and hands and knew that I smelled like part of it all, smelled right at home with the derelicts and failed souls. Here was self-pity, easy to put on, hard to relinquish, at the age of eighteen.

I remember the faces of the men that morning, a group of grotesques by Leonardo, with care and disillusionment lining the flaccid cheeks, the sneering, downturned lips. Self-pity; self-absorption; finally, self-hatred. I saw it all on the gray-lined skulls, in the bodies' cowering positions of sleep. We were animals in the yard, cringing at the blows of fate—and where there were no real blows, imagined blows would do. I watched a heavy body turn, its face for a moment casting a ragged profile against the brick. Fingers slowly scratched at lice or lust; urine ran down the creases of torn trousers; a cough bubbled up from the deep. Decay and waste refueled themselves. Against the floor of the cell, the calloused fingers of an unwashed fist opened and tapped in sleep against the cold surface. Nearby a head rocked back and forth and gave out a melody of spittle. Worms, I thought, worms are the only artists.

The cell groaned and I groaned with it, for I had nothing to be proud of in my life, and no one to whom I could make amends.

But there was paper in the cell, a pile of old newspapers, a roll of towels, and, next to the cell door, a pencil that dangled from a string.

Outside the window, the early-Sunday-morning sounds began a slow indistinct blurring. The jailhouse was on the same street as the Baptist church, and by standing on the ledge and hauling myself up, I could look out the barred window into the day: the blue morning fog burning off, the lights coming on in what looked like dollhouse windows, two old women who came out with buckets of water and sprinkled them on the dirt yard. I looked hard at the houses and the street, at the church women in their flowered hats and the youngsters who followed them along, sleepy-eyed and silent, the cars that started up with an angry pop, the clamor of small bells. I drew myself out of that filthy cell, until I was somewhere between the jailhouse and the church, somewhere invisible, where who I was and how I appeared didn't matter. I wasn't one place or the other, one thing or the other. Just a drawing on brown paper, curling at the edges.

In midafternoon I was released, and driven as far as the Iowa border by the sheriff's deputy. The old river was muddy and smug as I crossed over it, and the spring air was all complicity. My brother, little Christopher, and my dog came out to meet me, and their enthusiasm at the sight of me welcomed me home. Nearly a year gone by, a gulp of air held and held, and now exhaled.

That evening when Dad came home, I went and stood next to him in the yard at dusk while he watered the roses. In the year that had passed, he seemed to have grown even more solid; he was sturdy and thick as an elm, and no more loquacious. But I didn't mind the silence, was glad of the gentle whirring of the hawkmoths that hovered over the four-o'clocks.

"Your mother and I are glad you're home safe," he said, bending to straighten the stems of some waterlogged cosmos.

"I don't want to let the hair down my back," he said, "but I'll tell you this: your old dad did some things when he was younger that might surprise you."

I waited. The image of his graying Glenn Ford haircut cascading back over his shoulders was shocking. I waited, but he said no more. His tact, his reticence, filled the yard.

Back in my room, I drew and drew. Sex was all in my fingers now. Drawing was the way of making sense of the world. The drawings I'd done in my cell, with the dawn stinking around me, I put into a cardboard portfolio and stacked against my bedroom wall, with others: sketches of women holding babies, men and angels, plants that were animals and animals that were plants. I found I could turn realistic details to unrealistic effect; some were convoluted, some were simple. They were facts in the world, and as they existed I existed. Making art had before that spring seemed to me a means to something, a means to a style of life, to glory, but now it was more, it was a gift in itself. Drawing and loving. James had told me again and again in New Orleans to use my imagination, and now, finally, I did. Aspiration took a holiday, and I got down to simply getting by.

So the foolery of what I thought I ought to have been lay in shreds around me. Youth's resiliency cushioned me from the pain of not finding James where I'd left him; I saw that when I drank, his image came back most awfully, most clearly, and the pain then was the worst, so I stopped drinking. The house on Oak Street was too small for me, and I felt my arms and legs sticking out the windows, my head brushing the roof—but that was all right. I had learned to put my difference to use, and was thus relieved of it. I knew I wasn't like all the other young men and women I'd gone to school with in Lillienthal. The uniqueness I'd yearned for seemed real enough at home, but I'd learned that out in the wider world, it evaporated.

I decided to join the great throng of eighteen-year-old American buffalo thundering toward universities all across the land. Such a plan was what my family had hoped for, and now I saw no reason to go against it. I had something that the other students might not have been given, a sense of my own limits. But the limits made whatever talent I had all the more important.

I could begin by taking classes at my father's old alma mater, in the summer session, thus making up for the credits and the year I'd lost. I found I was undeterred by the prospect of a wholesome anonymous education. I was now quite sure who I was; never mind any more nonsense about who I was going to be.

I had been back home a month and was taking classes at Maquoketa College by the time my birthday arrived. As always happened, the day itself got subsumed by the larger event, the Fourth of July, two days later—but because I was so newly restored to family, my parents decided to make more out of the combined occasion than they did usually. They had, that spring, at last joined the country club, and we all dressed up for dinner at River Hills, where we were also to see the fireworks display that evening. Franklin brought along his new fiancée, Maureen, and Dennie Lee and Chris sat beside them, making up a table of five kings and two queens, as the club hostess pointed out, earning a chuckle for her ready smarm. Make that four kings, and hold the mayo.

The River Hills clubhouse had been elaborately decorated and festooned for the holiday: red-white-and-blue streamers and rosettes hung from the eaves and curled out of the centerpieces on each table in the dining room. The golfing crowd had acquired its leathery summer look, and talk rose up of birdies and handicaps, the newly annexed state of Hawaii. Jack Fleck, a local golfer who had once won the Western Open tournament, moved from table to table, sharing his celebrity, affable and stout. The body still ruled at River Hills, the well-oiled, well-scrubbed human apparatus, the sportsman. Our meal was punctuated by the sound of firecrackers exploding on distant fairways, women's laughter made higher and shriller by the air of festivity. The shrimp, the club rolls, and the ruddy roast beef leaped nimbly from serving cart to plate.

After the strawberry shortcake, there was dancing.

"I've heard so much about you," said Maureen as we moved out onto the floor. She was dark-eyed, dark-haired, with something of an impish grin. She and Franklin were to be married in October, she said, if they could wait that long. We danced to "Love Letters in the Sand," laughing at the putzers colliding. Franklin cut in, and they had a whirl together; I went back to our table and sat beside Mom. Her eyes followed the couple as they danced in and out of the bumptious crowd. Dad was talking to Jack Fleck about his grip; Dennie Lee and Chris were at the bar.

"I think they look awfully nice together, don't you?" She moved her head to the music. "All my boys can dance," she said, turning to smile at me. "It must be something in the genes."

I could see she was thinking of progeny, of Franklin and Maureen providing a swarm of little McGinnises. The future brood was as palpable as if it were out there dancing with them on the floor, dodging elbows and twirling with delight: faces that brought hers and Dad's into the future, short limbs that would grow long and fruitful themselves. The bodies on the dance floor multiplied, teeming with generation.

I stepped outside. The moon over the line of trees on the

eighteenth fairway seemed fat and wise and imperturb-able, like a Buddha rising in the sky, the pines beneath it black in silhouette. The night smelled of the clay along the riverbanks and the seed that was coming up in the fields, the voluptuousness of the earth was everywhere.

On the putting green, men preparing the fireworks display moved back and forth like shadows, carrying and securing pinwheels and spires. The wet smell of punk and ozone blended with the smell of the earth, the famil-iar odor of golf bags piled up beside the pro shop, leather and canvas, a whiff of chlorine from the swimming pool. I walked over to the deserted pool, bits of the moon wrin-kling and unwrinkling on its surface. And thought about my days there with Sammy, the nights spent in her em-brace along the fairways. An embrace, a warm cajoling—a long time ago.

I walked down the grassy slope to the green, thinking the line of men and trees there, the light and the dark, was something beautiful. A figure straightened from where it had been bending over a rocket, straightened and paused in its work to light a cigarette, the flame of the match for a moment illuminating the dark handsome face.

It was James's face. It was James.

He did not seem surprised to see me there, but it had never been his custom to show surprise. "How you been?" he asked, still cool as a cucumber, still sweet as molasses.

"Okay," I said. "And you?"

I guess I would have liked him to take me in his arms, or me to take him in mine—but that's not the way it went. We only stood there smiling and abashed under the moon.

"Gettin' along," he said, and readjusted the angle of the rocket. In the background his father, Horace, was lighting a string of sparklers on the apron of the green—a long line of letters in a word I couldn't discern, throwing off white sparks. The word was HAPPY, perhaps.

"I'm sorry," I said, "for being a fool. It was like running away, wasn't it? I'm sorry I was so stupid. I'm sorry I hurt you."

He said, "That's all right now."

He looked at his hands. I looked at the sky.

"I'm sorry too," he said, "for leaving you flat."

But it wasn't the two of us we were apologizing for—it was two boys who had ceased to be; we were two ghosts shining on the eighteenth green. My heart, which had been so full to see him, was empty.

"Where did you go . . . afterward?" I asked.

"Oh, up and down the river most of the summer. Then up to New York later on."

So we had been, all winter, as far apart as we could be on the same continent. "I went out to California," I said when he didn't ask.

"How was that?" he said with a dark smile that brought his beauty flooding in.

"One disaster after another. I tried to be an actor."

Over our heads now suddenly the sky was filled with thunderous cracks and a huge zinnia of orange lights. From the clubhouse nearby the first sounds of appreciation rose up like the rockets themselves.

"James," I said, in the short lull that followed. He lowered his head and looked at me. It seemed I saw his eyes soften for a moment. Then there was another flower in the sky, and he looked up again.

I had wanted to say, You must forgive me. You must love me—for I knew I still loved him. We will start over. Because otherwise my life is going to be a thing that doesn't work.

But the fireworks went on, filling up our eyes and ears. I stood there beside him, watching the lights above me, feeling the heat beside me.

"James," I said again. He was half-smiling up at the sky. He looked at me. "Mickey, I got my work to be doin'."

"Sure," I said. "Can I help?"

"You just stand clear while Horace and me get these things off the ground."

Horace had been moving along a line of rockets, lighting one at a time. Now he had reached the edge of the green. He saw me and nodded politely but with no particular sense of recollection. I stood out of the way as one by one James and his father lighted the short fuses. On other fairways other people were doing the same. Suddenly over the whole golf course jeweled flowers of light, flowers like universes, burst into being, showering us with radiance, rapturing my heart.

Afterword:
Michael's Room

Robert Ferro and Michael Grumley, known to their friends as the Ferro-Grumleys, or simply the F-Gs, lived in one of those rent-controlled apartments New Yorkers would sell their souls to have: a central hall, two nice bedrooms, a comfortable living room plus dining room, a decent kitchen and bath, and even a foyer with an ample closet for everyone's coat. The windows had only a second-floor view of a bricked alley, but for two writers with other landscapes to contemplate this was hardly a problem, and with so many things to admire inside, the visitor's gaze seldom strayed.

Treasures collected from countless places filled every space, including choice objects from Italy, the land of Robert's ancestors and Michael's historical fantasies. Prized among these Italian things were a thirties deco rug hung on one of the dining room walls, an exquisite Florentine desk lamp made entirely of wood that stood next to Robert's typewriter, two large Doric columns expertly done in faux marble, and the bust of a carnival fortune-teller, her eyes veiled in scarves, who presided over the living room, knew all, and said nothing.

143

Despite this Italian presence, the apartment had the feel less of a Tuscan villa than of a comfortably overstuffed English cottage, thanks to the plump sofa and chairs covered in a cheerful floral print and to the elaborate tea service that greeted visitors in the dining room. Two, sometimes three pots with fitted cozies would be on the table, along with cups and saucers of fine china, gleaming silverware, well-matched napkins, and, of course, a sumptuous display of cakes, delicate sandwiches, and other delights of the most irresistible kind. Tea at the Ferro-Grumleys' was a sacred ritual, perfected in every detail, and to be invited to tea, especially for the first time, was a social achievement to be savored.

Among the guests one might meet on different occasions were poet Richard Howard, composer Ned Rorem, critic Walter Clemons, editor Bill Whitehead, art historian James Saslow, fast-food heiress Margaret Sanders, journalist Stephen Greco, and his lover, dance critic Barry Laine. One would also find several novelists, including Julia Markus, Edmund White, Andrew Holleran, and Felice Picano. These last three, together with Robert, Michael, George Whitmore, and Christopher Cox, had formed the membership of The Violet Quill, an informal writing workshop that had met between the summer of 1979 and the winter of 1981 and had launched a new generation of gay novelists. Holleran had known the Ferro-Grumleys longest, since their student days in the late sixties at the University of Iowa Writers' Workshop. Robert and Michael had met there and fallen in love, beginning a relationship that was to last more than twenty-one years.

Apart from the cakes and tea, the most tempting item served during those late afternoons was gossip. Much of it was an exchange of artistic information: What play or biography was in the works? How successful was someone's new novel or collection of poems? What kinds of scenes were particularly maddening to write? And some of it was the sheer business of publishing: the virtues of various editors and agents, the size of advances and print runs, publicity budgets, paperback rights, movie rights— all interesting enough subjects made fascinating by Robert's and Michael's inexhaustible passion for them. We learned again that the world was filled with inequities, that it was an unpredictable place where talent was often ignored while a few got more fame, money, and even sex than they deserved. It was at one of these teas that a newborn star of gay letters was delightedly branded with the name Eve Harrington, after the ambitious young actress in *All About Eve*.

Tea was a ritual the Ferro-Grumleys practiced wherever they went, with or without guests, in their own residence or someone else's. When they visited me for weekends on Long Island, they paid no attention to my protests that we could hardly be hungry for a meticulously prepared dinner at eight if we gorged ourselves on sugary pastries from five to six. They believed, quite simply, that one could always eat. They had their tea in the many apartments they rented in Rome and during each of the long summer days they spent at the Ferro family beachhouse on the New Jersey coast—a house made famous by Robert in his novels and affectionately known to the rest of us as Gaywyck-sur-mer. Whether in New York, Rome, or New Jersey, Robert awoke every morning at seven, worked at his typewriter, began preparing Michael's breakfast at ten-thirty, and served it promptly at eleven—

the unvarying moment of Michael's *levée*. In their world there always seemed to be a consecrated time and place for everything.

We all knew that these rituals were the result of a long process of accommodation by which two men of strong wills and complex temperaments had worked out a way to live together, had made themselves a home. As in other couples, there had been jealousies, infidelities, and moments when each had wondered whether it was worth going on, but they had found solutions and made affirmations. We felt this history when we assembled for tea, and we understood that every object in that apartment had its own intimate story related to its discovery, its purchase, and the place that had been chosen for it next to all the other objects of a shared life. We joked about the Ferro-Grumleys' being such creatures of habit, yet the feeling they conveyed to their guests and friends was one of peace, hard won perhaps and based on innumerable compromises but also built firmly on respect and a very deep love. Thanks to this peace, they possessed the most precious commodity of all: the time for each to perform the solitary task of writing.

Their ordered life also served to balance, and possibly to justify, their abiding lust for adventure. They had known each other for little more than a year when, inspired by one of Edgar Cayce's prophecies, they set sail for the Bahamas on the Ferro family's boat to find the lost continent of Atlantis. The strange underwater structures they discovered and the book they wrote together, *Atlantis: The Autobiography of a Search* (1970), made them famous enough to give them both a lasting, if often disappointed, faith in literary glory. It also confirmed their shared vision of the world as a place of multiple realities existing wondrously together in time and space.

Michael built quickly on the success of *Atlantis* by writing three works of nonfiction: *There Are Giants in the Earth* (1974), about Big Foot and related phenomena; *Hard Corps* (1976), a detailed study of the homosexual and heterosexual S/M subculture; and *After Midnight* (1978), a beautiful series of portraits of people who work at night that received praise from Studs Terkel and the offer of a movie option for the last chapter about Gloria, a New York actress and belly dancer. Although the movie was never made, when I first met the Ferro-Grumleys during a Gay Pride parade in New York in 1979, Michael was definitely the better known of the two.

For more than a decade after the publication of *Atlantis*, Robert was admired by a happy few as the author of *The Others* (1977), his mysterious and brilliantly conceived novel about a group of characters on a ship searching for a reality where they can fully come to life. Then, in the eighties, Robert wrote three novels in succession: *The Family of Max Desir* (1983), *The Blue Star* (1985), and *Second Son* (1988). *Max* established Robert's reputation as an important novelist, particularly because of his uncompromising examination of the gay man's role within the traditional family. The struggle over the issue of homosexuality that pits Max and his lover Nick against Max's conservative Catholic father is similar to the fight Robert and Michael waged to have their own relationship unconditionally accepted by the Ferro family.

Both men believed that the homosexual's paradoxical situation of being at once an outsider and an insider made him a potentially keen observer of the contradictions and hypocrisies of society. The gay man could be the truth-sayer of the family and, by extension, of humanity itself. Robert articulated these views forcefully at the time of the publication of *Second Son*. Why are there homosexuals? he asked. Where do we belong? What do we have that makes us able to contribute to the tribe? His answer was that the "otherness" of homosexuality, its own otherworldliness, gave gay men, and especially gay artists, a kind of sha-manistic access to alternative existences and a special knowledge of death. In Robert's novels these other worlds become tales within tales, counterfictions that play with and against the more realistic narrative on the surface and give it a fascinating resonance. In *The Blue Star* he de-scribes the secrets of a Masonic temple hidden beneath Central Park, and in *Second Son* the gay planet Splendora offers hope to men afflicted with AIDS.

This "spirituality," as Robert called it, had a variety of sources, some of them rather suspect to the rest of us. The Ferro-Grumleys believed in the magical power of various trinkets in their apartment. They read the works of Edgar Cayce and consulted numerous clairvoyants or "witches" in Rome, finally settling on a man who predicted that one of them would die of cancer in his late forties. Michael himself was a devout Buddhist who wrote letters to the Dalai Lama. Yet none of this was ever frivolous. Their hunger to explore other worlds was such that all their works may be seen as children of their first book, *Atlantis*, and everything they wrote, together or separately, could bear the title "The Autobiography of a Search," particu-larly when that search led them to penetrate the mysteries of their own fears and passions. Although *Life Drawing* is firmly grounded in the often brutal realities of everyday existence, it is also part of this shared spiritual vision.

The decisions that led Michael to his novel were difficult ones. Despite their seemingly comfortable life, the Ferro-Grumleys never had much money and had to allot their meager resources with great care. Just as Robert had found a job during the seventies to give Michael the time to write his books, so Michael worked following the publication of *After Midnight* to support Robert's writing and give him "his turn." If there were problems in this arrangement, we never heard of them, but it did seem to most of us that by 1985 Michael's star was fading while Robert was getting ever more attention from his growing public. A few suggested that their relationship might not survive the strain.

The truth is, Michael never stopped writing. Following a long-established practice, he made daily entries in his journal that would someday amount to more than twenty volumes of manuscript. He began a regular column in the *New York Native* called "Uptown" in which he covered an impressive range of cultural events and seasoned his comments with sharp observations on the passing foibles of metropolitan life. He also did considerable work on a novel entitled *A World of Men*, an excerpt from which was published as "Public Monuments" in Felice Picano's anthology of lesbian and gay writing *A True Likeness* (1980). Finally, Michael continued to do his beautiful drawings, which reminded us that he was also an accomplished artist who had studied at the School of Visual Arts and designed the covers of several books, including Robert's *The Others* and Robert Peters's *What Dillinger Meant to Me*.

By 1984 he had assembled many of his drawings and texts into a collection called "The Way of the Animals," a sensitive Buddhist-Taoist vision of nature that was considered by several publishers but eventually dropped because of the prohibitive costs of reproducing the artwork. Michael was profoundly disappointed.

It was also in 1984 that my friendship with Robert and Michael became much stronger. I was involved in putting together the first *Men on Men* collection of gay fiction and had asked Robert for a contribution. Since I saw Michael primarily as a writer of nonfiction, I did not consider asking him until Felice Picano urged me to do so. Felice expected Michael to give me another piece from *A World of Men*, but what I received was a section from an extensively revised draft of the novel now titled *Life Drawing*. I liked the story immediately. As in "Public Monuments," one of its themes was the unpredictability of life, especially the way sexual desire could go out of control, causing pain and violence. Now, however, the protagonist was not a American man in Rome, but an adolescent from Iowa who runs away from home and, like Huckleberry Finn, sails down the Mississippi on a barge, where he falls in love with a young black man whose trust he eventually betrays through sexual infidelity. It was a finely written, dramatic, and surprisingly moral tale about the loss of innocence, as well as an exceptionally sensitive portrait of an interracial relationship. It was also one of the messiest manuscripts I have ever read.

Hating computers and eager to save money, Michael revised his typewritten work by erasing unwanted words or phrases before typing over the spaces with new material. Unfortunately, after photocopying, one could never be sure if the ghostly words in these spaces were from the poorly erased original version or from the badly reproduced revision. "Michael, we have to talk," I told him, and within a few days we were sitting together, manuscript in hand, on that plump floral sofa. I was a fledgling editor and feared the worst, but except for one objection, Michael listened quietly for more than an hour as I pointed out problems and made suggestions for additional revisions. I know we became friends that day because the next time I visited for tea, Michael took me aside and showed me his room for the first time.

It was the smaller of the two bedrooms and appeared to have space for little more than a narrow bed, a shallow desk, and a large screen extending diagonally across the floor. I don't think Michael ever slept there, except possibly for naps, since the other bedroom had a bed big enough for the two of them. But this was his room, an extension of his mind and body, and it protected his special treasures. I didn't know that day how much was there. No one knew until after the apartment had to be emptied. Then Robert's sisters opened the closet and found an entire collection of groovy sixties clothes—high-collared shirts in multiple colors, hiphuggers with wide bell-bottoms, fancy shoes with thick heels. They looked under the bed and discovered trunks like pirates' chests filled with papers—the volumes of Michael's journal, his drawings, the manuscripts of all his books and essays, clippings from innumerable magazines and newspapers from the *New York Times* to the *Asbury Park Press*. Many pages had yellowed, almost melted into each other as in a thick palimpsest. And in shirt pockets, books, and the hidden corners of the trunks they found money, more than eighty dollars in singles and silver saved for a rainy day perpetually postponed.

What struck me most when I entered Michael's room was that it was a shrine, or rather the site of two shrines for two extraordinary beings—the Buddha and the Afro-American Male. On a table next to his desk Michael had assembled a collection of Buddhas, a large statue surrounded by smaller ones that were in turn circled by tiny figures of animals, each representing a year in the Chinese calendar. Fresh flower petals completed the altar. Michael showed me the responses he had received to his letters from one of the Dalai Lama's retainers. They were written on beautiful stationery stamped with the official seal and contained invitations for Michael and his friend to come to tea at Dharmsala.

The other shrine was something else altogether. We had always known that Robert's and Michael's strong erotic attraction to Afro-American men had occasionally caused problems in their relationship. We also knew that over time they had become politically committed to justice for people of color everywhere. During a dinner in Boston I had witnessed them verbally demolish a man who had dared support the white viewpoint on apartheid. And in his column, "Uptown," Michael had written so naturally about black and Hispanic cultural events in Harlem that many of his readers when first meeting him were surprised to see he was Caucasian. Yet none of this prepared me for what I saw in Michael's room. Pictures of Afro-American men covered the four panels of the screen and surrounded the single window. There were photographs, drawings, images cut from newspapers and magazines of men of every physical type and skin color and from a variety of occupations—athletes, workers, businessmen, models, poets. Most were clothed, a few naked, none anonymous. Not only did Michael have several photographs that were signed and dedicated to him, but he knew the names and biographies of every man there.

That afternoon I realized the source of Michael's remarkable sensitivity to people of color and his ability to portray them so convincingly in his work. From downtrodden workers to fancy gamblers, the black characters in *Life Drawing* are as richly diverse as their white counterparts. Utterly real yet endowed with wonder, they assume exemplary positions of wretchedness and dignity, violence and order, dissipation and morality. Like gays in a straight world, they are at once similar to the rest of society and different because of an otherness that is less a form of alienation than an invitation to adventure and knowledge. They, too, are guides and truthsayers.

By the spring of 1987 Michael had completed a full draft of *Life Drawing* and was ready to send it to publishers. The section that had appeared in *Men on Men* the preceding fall had been so well received that he decided to open the novel with it, changing the chronological order of the narrative. There was even talk that *Life Drawing* might be published soon after Robert's *Second Son*, giving them both a banner year nearly two decades after *Atlantis*. Then everything changed. More of us learned what a few had already known—that Robert had been suffering from Kaposi's sarcoma for more than four years. Michael's willingness to support his lover's writing took on a new meaning: Robert might die before finishing his work.

Once *Second Son* had gone to press, they returned to Rome that winter and rented an apartment high above the Piazza Navona. Michael had been granted access to the Vatican Library to do research on his next book, a historical novel on the excesses of the sixteenth-century papacy. They planned to savor their second home in the Eternal City more than ever, but Michael's health, not Robert's, suddenly declined. He started having headaches, nausea, crushing fatigue. He reacted poorly to medication. Although several expressed interest, no publisher seemed ready to sign a contract for the novel. They returned to the old apartment on West Ninety-fifth Street, and Robert curtailed the book tour he had carefully planned for *Second Son*. Almost as bad as the illness we saw on Michael's face was his look of discouragement. He seemed pursued by the same sense of failure that haunts his young hero in *Life Drawing*.

By February Michael was in the New York University Medical Center receiving treatment for a growing number of opportunistic infections. Robert got them a room in the cooperative care unit with a spectacular view of Manhattan and moved in. He left only to give a few readings from *Second Son* and to use all his influence to push for the publication of *Life Drawing*. He was convinced that the acceptance of the novel would give Michael the moral boost necessary to reverse his decline. The rest of us paid visits, ran errands, and tried to satisfy Michael's sudden cravings for cheeseburgers or pizza, but in the last days he was unable to recognize anyone, not even Robert. He died on March 28, 1988.

Robert's health never recovered from the exhaustion of caring for his lover. With all the energy he had left he gave himself now to the final things. He planned every detail of Michael's memorial service and selected a site for their ashes on a bluff overlooking the Hudson River in Rockland County. He chose a white marble stone that would be inscribed with the same words as the epigraph to *Life Drawing*—"Love is a babe" from Shakespeare's Sonnet 115. He spoke to friends of his desire to establish a foundation in his name and Michael's to reward outstanding works of fiction on gay and lesbian life. And he made every effort to give *Life Drawing* its best chance at publication. After considerable deliberation he cut a few redundancies and added a dozen lines from Michael's own draft of a revision of the novel's ending. More important, he restored the original chronological order of the narrative, thereby bringing the novel closer to what Michael had always intended it to be—a bildungsroman of the American road, the story of a young man's search for an identity and a home. Robert survived his lover by ten weeks. He died on July 11, 1988.

Since that time the Ferro-Grumley Foundation has been established, and it gave its first awards in 1990. The Beinecke Library at Yale University will be acquiring the papers of writers who belonged to The Violet Quill, including Michael's voluminous journal. These papers will form the core of a growing gay archives that will support future study and research. And now, more than three years after Michael's death, *Life Drawing* has been published just the way he would have wanted—in cloth, a picture of him and Robert on the jacket. I am very fond of this photograph taken by Robert Giard in 1985. I like my friends' eyes, their hands, and the way their gestures mirror each other on either side of that famous faux marbled column. They are lovers, unquestionably, but I also see in them the young men who went off to search for Atlantis, and who remained what they always were—seductive devils, beautiful pirates.

GEORGE STAMBOLIAN
April 1991